PRAISE FOR RODRIGO REY ROSA

SO-CFH-095

"I am an assiduous reader of Rodrigo Rey Rosa. . . . To read his work is to learn to write, and it is also an invitation to the pure pleasure of being swept away by his sinister and fantastic narratives."

ROBERTO BOLAÑO

"Rodrigo Rey Rosa has developed a signature prose style . . . achieving a poetic elegance that is both lucid and precise."

RICARDO BAIXERAS, *elPeriodico.com*

"[Rodrigo Rey Rosa's] prose is almost elliptical, full of sharp turns immersed in fleeting sensory, impressionistic shadows."

CLAUDE-MICHEL CLUNY, *Le Figaro Litteraire*

"Rodrigo Rey Rosa's prose, dense and precise, shows his literary relationship to legendary writer Paul Bowles."

DER SPIEGEL

"[Rodrigo Rey Rosa's] writing shows a prose style laid completely bare, in a way in which there is no superfluous word. . . . [His narratives] are consuming and sensual to the point of obsessiveness, almost like lived dreams."

PERE GIMFERRER

"The Guatemalan writer focuses his energy, certainly, on the subtle elements of his style: the speed, exactitude, and concise beauty of his prose, combined with the elliptical flow of his narratives, continue to recommend him as a young master in the art of saying more with less."

GUSTAVO GUERRERO, *Letras Libres*

"Each new book by Rodrigo Rey Rosa . . . [has] the special quality of a meticulous prose, elaborate to the point of being handcrafted, though not in search of style, but rather, on the contrary, of writing that is refined, light, silent—that is evocative and imaginative rather than informative."

J. A. MASOLIVER RÓDENAS, *La Vanguardia*

"Rey Rosa creates narratives of mythic proportions."

SAN FRANCISCO CHRONICLE

PRAISE FOR *LA ORILLA AFRICANA* (THE AFRICAN SHORE)

"*La orilla africana* is expertly designed; it raises a series of small and large questions, which relay one another cunningly, maintaining narrative tension up to the haunting conclusion, and indeed beyond. . . . It is tempting to call *La orilla africana* a minimalist novel, because of its scaled-down look, but that would be misleading. Although it systematically avoids emphasis, it touches on large and urgent themes."

CHRIS ANDREWS, *The Quarterly Conversation*

"In *La orilla africana*, Rodrigo Rey Rosa attempts a literature of the senses and of fundamental understanding. I don't mean to refer to Rey Rosa's as experimental literature, but rather to note its author's use of literature as a sensual and moral sense. And by use, I mean, of reading to the point of almost irrational enjoyment."

ERNESTO AYALA-DIP, *El Correo Español*

"With a style both diaphanous and precise, at once strong and delicate, in *La orilla africana* events are never premeditated. . . . The success of the novel is above all in underscoring, without sensationalism, how fate welcomes [the characters]."

JOSE CARLOS CATAÑO, *ABC Madrid*

"The clarity of the fabric [Rey Rosa] weaves in *La orilla africana* takes the reader off guard: we fail to leave the book, seduced as we are by an undefined suspense. The enigma lies here in its transparency."

CLAUDE-MICHEL CLUNY, *Le Figaro Litteraire*

"A show of stylistic restraint."

IGNACIO ECHEVARRÍA, *Babelia*

"We discover here [Rey Rosa] as a master of insinuation, of indirect allusion. He leaves much unsaid, leaving the imagination of the reader to read between the lines."

KLAUS JETZ, *Entwicklungspolitik*

"The promising progress and development of Rodrigo Rey Rosa as a writer that some critics awaited in 1994 has now been completed."

RAQUEL LUZÁRRAGA, *Quimera*

"Light as can be, Rey Rosa's prose seems to emerge straight from a long alembic in which it has been distilled, as if the events of the narrative tell themselves, without any manipulation."

JAVIER APARICIO MAYDEU, *El Periódico*

"Rey Rosa writes in a very precise and very fresh style. He recounts what the characters do, but above all, what they see and what they perceive. [The book] breathes life."

VALENTIN SCHÖNHERR, *Lateinamerika Nachrichten*

The
African
Shore

The African Shore

Shore

(La orilla africana)

RODRIGO REY ROSA

TRANSLATED BY JEFFREY GRAY

YALE UNIVERSITY PRESS ■ NEW HAVEN & LONDON

A MARGELLOS
WORLD REPUBLIC OF LETTERS BOOK

The Margellos World Republic of Letters is dedicated to making literary works from around the globe available in English through translation. It brings to the English-speaking world the work of leading poets, novelists, essayists, philosophers, and playwrights from Europe, Latin America, Africa, Asia, and the Middle East to stimulate international discourse and creative exchange.

Published with assistance from the foundation established in memory of Calvin Chapin of the Class of 1788, Yale College.

Yale University Press books may be purchased in quantity for educational, business, or promotional use. For information, please e-mail sales.press@yale.edu (U.S. office) or sales@yaleup.co.uk (U.K. office).

Set in Electra and Nobel types by Keystone Typesetting, Inc.
Printed in the United States of America.

Library of Congress Cataloging-in-Publication Data
Rey Rosa, Rodrigo, 1958–
[Orilla Africana. English]
The African shore / Rodrigo Rey Rosa ; Translated by Jeffrey Gray.
   pages   cm — (A Margellos world republic of letters book)
Originally published as La Orilla Africana. F&G Editores.
ISBN 978-0-300-19610-8 (alk. paper)
I. Title.
PQ7499.2.R38O713 2013
863'.64—dc23   2013007483

A catalogue record for this book is available from the British Library.

This paper meets the requirements of ANSI/NISO Z39.48-1992 (Permanence of Paper).

10 9 8 7 6 5 4 3 2 1

CONTENTS

Part One

THE COLD

I

It was still dark when Hamsa got up, and the wind out of the east was whistling over the cliff face, rattling the branches and leaves like a thousand maracas. He could hear the waves crashing violently on the rocks at the foot of the cliff. He finished his ablutions, then knelt to pray on the skin of a sheep slaughtered at the last Aid el Kebir. He brewed a glass of tea on his small brazier, broke open a dark round loaf of bread, and dunked a piece of it in a dish of olive oil. "In God's name," he said, and began to eat.

It was just getting light when he set out toward the slopes of Shlokía, where he had last seen the stray lamb just before returning to the sheep cote the day before. He followed the road along the cliff, the frogs still croaking around him, and passed below a big abandoned house that had once belonged to the Perdicaris family. Instead of following the path through the pine woods, he chose a trail through the thickets where he had found other strays in the past. Raising his arms from time to time against the thorns, he moved inward through a dim tunnel of vegetation. It was dangerous here, he knew—he could easily run into a wild boar—but he wasn't afraid. He knew no *djinn* would come here: the *djinn* hated thorns (which was why Muslims let thorns grow on their family graves). The thicket was damp with dew, and inside it stank of resin, rosemary, and porcupine droppings.

Beyond the wide swath of bushes lay the shore with its big boulders and punishing waves over which a cold wind buffeted the seagulls back and forth. Hamsa cried out twice for the lamb, looking carefully down the slope as the first rays of daylight gilded the sides of the rocks. Nothing. He climbed up to the little grove that concealed the ruins of the old Spanish boating club, and looked into what had once been the swimming pool, now ruined and overgrown with grass. Nothing. Finally, he climbed back down to the steep rocks where the sea was pounding.

He was standing next to a rock wall when he saw the lamb a few meters below him, cornered between two boulders, splashed intermittently by the waves; it was trembling. How had it gotten there? Maybe some of the soldiers' dogs had chased it— they had their barracks near the boating club. He began to ease himself down, sliding dangerously along the wall, his body pressed to the sandy rock. He was seized with an irrepressible shiver, the way one is when scaling the trunk of a very tall tree. His foot searched blindly for support in a chink of the rock but couldn't find one. His sweaty hands locked for a moment onto a sharp outcropping. Suddenly, a turtledove flew close behind him. Hamsa turned his head with a shudder, and the rock came off in his hand with a dull crack. He landed feet first on the rocks below, a stab of pain in his heel. He looked around him.

"*Yalatif!*"

His fall had sent the lamb tumbling into the sea.

Without taking his eyes off the animal, its little white head bobbing in the waves, Hamsa quickly stripped off his gandura, his Nikes, and his drawers. Calling out God's name, he jumped into the water.

II

Hamsa had been smoking kif since he was a child. His grandmother Fátima tried to get him to quit, going so far as to sprinkle drops of urine on the kif, but it was no use. Hamid, his father, now dead, laughed the day Fátima told him how she had surprised Hamsa stealing kif from his sheep-bladder pouch as he slept.

"A chip off the old block," he said.

Hamsa smoked kif every day when he herded for Si Mohammed M'rabati, who had hundreds of sheep, and who liked the idea that they pastured on the slopes of Agla, which lay between Tangier and Cape Spartel. Sitting on a flat rock, watching the sea in the mouth of the strait, Hamsa would play his lyre to relax after a pipe. Sometimes he would go down as far as the Sinduq, a giant rock shaped like a coffer half-sunk in the sea, to see the creamy blue water rise and fall among the honey- and cinnamon-colored boulders. But he usually couldn't smoke there. The east wind or the north wind would pick the kif right up and scatter it over the water, where it might stir up the dreadful beings who lived under the waves and who could bring bad luck. You could get sick and have impure thoughts. Like when Hamsa had to pass a night in the *quba*, the tomb of Sidi Mesmudi, which is in Monte Viejo, because he had caught typhus. The next morning he saw a woman give a black chicken to an old man with a yellow turban. He watched the old man draw a knife from under his shirt, call upon Allah, and, crouching next to the saint's fountain, cut the animal's throat. Or like when he had sullied himself with a sheep, hiding behind a black canvas lean-to, wishing all the while that the sheep would turn into a woman but thankful that God had at least ordered things in such a way that the sheep didn't get pregnant. Or like when he plunged his penis into a pile of donkey dung to make it grow bigger.

III

He opened his eyes. The sky was liquid blue, and the cold, though not as intense as he had expected, was countless needles and bubbles stuck to his skin. He spit salt water and blinked, looking for the lamb. Two strokes and he reached it. It had a fibrous little body, incredibly heavy for its size. Hamsa's head sank under a wave, and he felt a sharp sting of salt in his nostrils and a sourness in his throat, but he managed to get the animal to float. He paddled hard to keep it up above the rough surface of the water, as it churned back and forth between the boulders. With his free arm he struggled to approach the shore without being thrown against the rocks. He clutched at the foot of the large rock he had leapt from and rested a moment in a crevice, precariously shielded from the violence of the waves. He slung the lamb over his shoulders and crept up the rock as far as the landing where he had stripped off his clothes. The wind, coming in gusts from above, whistled and made the chill bone-deep. The lamb trembled uncontrollably, like an electric toy, in the little puddle of water draining from its wool; a ray of sunlight grazed its back as Hamsa stood at its side, taking the same ray full on his face.

"*Hamdul-láh*," he said, but at this moment the wind lifted up his pile of clothes, which lay one step away from him on the rock. They traced a downward arc into the sea.

"*Shaitán!*"

Hamsa leapt into the water again.

IV

On the way back to the hut, the lamb over his shoulders, Hamsa thought of his uncle Jalid, who was living in Spain. The last time his uncle had come to visit, he had given him the (imitation) Nikes he now wore constantly. They were the envy of Ismail, his playmate. Ismail was going to envy him all his life, because, as his uncle had said, Hamsa would be rich and would own lands and livestock. His father had died poor, and when Hamsa grew up, he would have to support his grandparents, Fátima and Artifo, who worked as servants in a house owned by a Christian woman in Monte Viejo.

"You want to have money, don't you?" his uncle said.

Hamsa reflected.

"Yes," he said.

And his uncle explained how, working for him, he would begin to earn money. It was an easy job, but only Hamsa could do it, because he knew that part of the coast better than anyone besides his uncle, who from childhood had been a shepherd like Hamsa, and, later, a fisherman. (It was a dangerous coast, lined with reefs and rocks, and full of steep cliffs and slopes covered with all sorts of vegetation, soaked incessantly by the sea wind.)

Before going back to Spain, his uncle visited the hut where Hamsa lived. Little Ismail was there, helping Hamsa mark the sheep they would sell that Sunday in the market.

"*Bghit n'hadar m'ak*," said his uncle. "I want to talk to you."

Hamsa told Ismail to get lost, and the boy ran out and disappeared behind some rocks. The uncle sat down on a stool that Hamsa kept in the shadow of a twisted fig tree, and Hamsa squatted in front of him, wiping the grime off his hands on the folds of his gandura.

"*Iyeh?*"

Was Hamsa ready to do the work? All his uncle asked was that Hamsa watch a certain part of the coast during one night. A speedboat with Jalid in it would approach the coast from Cádiz, and Hamsa would have to send signals with a lantern. Was Hamsa capable of spending the whole night awake, alert, so that no one, neither gendarmes nor soldiers patrolling the beach, would surprise them?

Of course he could do it, Hamsa said. He was already thinking of the various ways he knew to fight off sleep, like eating red ants or the dirt of an ant hill, drinking water with lice, or wearing an amulet made from an owl's eye.

"I knew I could count on you," his uncle told him. "You're a winner. You'll have cars and as many women as you want—even though they really cause a lot of problems." He smiled.

Jalid returned to Spain a few days later, and before long he sent news to Hamsa. They would decide soon on the exact date and place.

V

. It was nearly noon and the wind had almost dried his clothes when he set the lamb on the ground beside the fig tree. It shook itself violently and sneezed. Then it ran toward the corral of rocks and thorns to be near the flock and stood trembling against the fence in a patch of sunlight.

Hamsa went into the hut, blew on the embers that were still glowing in the brazier, and began to prepare his tea. Then he went out into the sun and sat down under the fig tree with his kif pipe. But smoking soon gave him a light headache, and Hamsa knew he had been struck by the *berd*, the cold that could pierce one to the bone. The wind was still blowing cold and hard; it had grown worse since sunrise.

In the afternoon, he took the flock as far as the pasture at the foot of the ruined house. He carried his lyre with him, but he didn't play it. Water flowed from his nostrils.

When the sun went down behind the mountain, Hamsa began to drive the flock back to the corral.

—*Derrrrrr! Derrrrrr!*

After counting the animals, he boiled some sheep's milk in a saucepan, drank a little, and fell asleep on a cushion of sheepskins, covered with a woolen shawl. Later, stretched out in the darkness, he felt the bite of the cold in all his bones. The sound of the wind nauseated him. He woke several times with the sensation that he was falling. He sank into his sickness. What would happen if his uncle called for him this very day? he wondered.

He woke up late, after dawn, drenched in sweat. When Ismail lifted the curtain of the hut to look inside, the daylight blinded Hamsa.

"Are you sick?" asked Ismail. "What's the matter?"

Hamsa sat up.

"The cold."

The boy came inside and sat down next to him. He kept looking at him in silence.

"What shall we do?" he asked.

Hamsa opened and closed his eyes.

"You know what would do you good?" said Ismail. "Some milk with pennyroyal."

"I've got milk here. Do you know where to get pennyroyal?"

"No." The boy stood up.

"Go and ask for a handful from my grandmother."

When the boy had gone, Hamsa sank back into a dream. A battle of swords that turned out to be bulrushes or reeds, then a rain of pebbles.

"*Aulidi*," said the voice of his grandmother, but she was not speaking to him. "Go tell Si Mohammed that Hamsa is sick and that he should send someone to look after the sheep. I'm going home now to talk with madame (who wouldn't mind putting him up for a few days, they knew how generous she was) and I'll be back in a taxi for him."

Ismail did not move. He stared at her with an expression that the old woman understood.

"Ah, you want money. Here, a hundred francs." She dropped a coin in the boy's little hand, which closed on it quickly.

VI

In the tool shed where they made a bed for him, Hamsa spent two days burning with fever. His grandmother made him drink milk with pennyroyal, fed him pennyroyal couscous, and rubbed his body with sheep grease, to which also she added pennyroyal powder.

"Drink this, my son. You'll be better soon."

Mohammed had sent Ismail to tell Hamsa not to worry, that old Larbi would take care of the flock while he was gone. Mohammed also sent fifty dirhams to pay for medicine, but Fátima didn't think much of the medicine of the Nazarenes, and she put away the money for future needs.

On the third morning, still weak and painfully stiff in his neck and shoulders, Hamsa stood up and took a few steps around the room. Later, he went out into the garden. The east wind was blowing hard as ever, and the sky was clear. The sun, mirrored a thousand times in the leaves, hurt his eyes so much he quickly went back inside to the comfort of the darkness.

At noon, his grandfather brought him chicken stew and sat down to have lunch with him.

"Now you're better," he said. "Tomorrow you'll go back to work." He drew from his jacket Hamsa's *motui*, the kit containing his pipe and kif, and put it on the mat with a gesture of tolerant disapproval. "Ismail brought this for you."

In the afternoon, when the light was softer and the wind had calmed, Hamsa went out into the garden again. He sat down in a raised section near an old monkey tree that grew on the other side of a bed of lilies. From there, behind the cane fence in the lower part of the garden, he could see the white hills of Tangier and the ocean. He watched a woman come out of the little guest house at the far end of the garden. He stopped smoking. She wore blue jeans and a white shirt, and her long blond hair was loose and damp. She wasn't young, but she wasn't old either. She crossed the garden by the flagstone path and turned into the main house. Hamsa smoked another pipe of kif. Now a man, who could have been Moroccan but who, judging by his clothes and way of walking, must have been European, came out of the guest house and followed the woman's steps up the gravel path. "Whore," Hamsa thought. A little later he could hear Madame Choiseul's car start and Fátima's voice shout at Artifo to open the gate. The noise of the car faded as it went down toward the city, and Hamsa took up his pipe again, dreaming that he was a rich man and that the garden was his.

THE OWL'S EYES

VII

The garden was deserted now. A crane, very white in the afternoon sun, had perched next to the Nazarene's lion's-head fountain. It flew off when Hamsa walked down the path toward the guest house. Hamsa circled the house, came up to a window, and peered inside. He saw an owl perched on the back of a chair with a carpet of newspapers spread under it. The owl, which had a fallen wing, seemed to be asleep. Hamsa tapped the pane with his finger. The owl turned its head around and looked at him.

"Yuuk," the owl said to Hamsa. "Yuuk."

Everyone knew that owls don't sleep at night and that they can see in the dark. This was why, when someone wanted to stay awake all night, it was a good idea to catch an owl and pull out its eyes. Some people boiled the eyes in water and ate them, or you could make an amulet with one of the eyes and wear it on your chest to keep off sleep.

Hamsa returned to the tool shed and smoked several pipes of kif, thinking of what he should do.

VIII

He came out of the tool shed and, making a wide circle, headed back toward the guest house. He carried a bundle of cord to tie up the owl with, and a two-handled basket full of firewood. The muezzin at the new mosque called out the evening prayer. Down among the many-colored trunks of the eucalypti, Hamsa saw his grandfather prostrate on his straw mat, concentrated in prayer. He headed down the flagstone path, glancing back once toward the main house, where there was no one in sight. But he couldn't be sure: the windows of Mme. Choiseul's room looked out on that part of the garden, and in the afternoon light they were large mirrors, reflecting the sky and the tops of the cypresses. The old Christian woman might be there. Hamsa hesitated a moment; then, saying *"Bismil-láh,"* he pushed open the door of the guest house and closed it quickly behind him.

The owl turned its head to look at Hamsa. It raised its good wing and opened its beak.

Hamsa advanced with the bundle of cord in one hand and the basket of kindling in the other. He lowered the basket to the floor, took out the kindling, and put it in a wicker container next to the fireplace. He approached the owl and saw its broken wing. He seized it by the neck, tied its feet—the owl did not resist—and put it in the two-handled basket. He looked around, approached the window, and opened it all the way. A cold wind entered the room.

IX

Old Larbi, smoking kif under the fig tree, scarcely opened his eyes when Hamsa appeared from behind the hut with the owl hidden in a bundle of clothes.

"*Salaam aleikum.*"

"*Aleikum salaam.*"

Larbi stood up, went into the hut for his things, and prepared to leave. He was a bad-humored old man. Hamsa thought Larbi doubted he was sick.

"The animals didn't give you any problem?"

"No."

"Where's Ismail?"

"I haven't seen him. He hasn't come by."

"If you see him, please tell him to come. I'm going to need his help."

The old man smiled mockingly. "*Ouakha*," he said. He turned and started up the road.

Hamsa went into the hut and took the owl out of the bundle of clothes. He drove a Y-shaped stake in the earth in one corner. He tied the cord to the stake to secure the owl. The owl hopped onto the Y and opened its beak.

Hamsa lay down on the sheepskins and filled a pipe with kif, waiting for Ismail to come.

"I'm cured now," he said when Ismail came in.

The little boy looked at the owl, perched on the Y, eyes closed, wing fallen.

"I'm going to kill it one of these days and eat one of its eyes," explained Hamsa. "With the other eye, I'll make an amulet."

Ismail seemed impressed.

"Poor thing."

"Come here," said Hamsa, making a downward gesture with his hand.

When the little boy stepped within reach, Hamsa grabbed one of his arms and pulled him toward him. With his free hand he lifted up his gandura.

Part Two

SKULLS

X

A sharp pain at the top of his head made him open his eyes. He rolled over in the sheets, remembering he was in a hotel called Atlas but unable to remember where he'd spent the last hours of the night before.

Those recent memories were lost forever in a hole of black light, but he knew that, once again, he had had too much to drink. Shaking his head no, he sat up on the edge of the bed. He picked up the phone to call his traveling mates, Victor and Ulysses, but they didn't answer. The receptionist told him they hadn't come back yet.

He stood up, walked to the window, and drew back the blood-colored curtains. He immediately regretted it. The clear African noon struck his eyes as if two fingers had jabbed through them all the way to the back of his head. He walked back to the bed and fell onto it, burying his head between the pillows.

Suddenly, he remembered—a memory in red and black, in miniature: two girls. They were laughing in shadows of muddy light, smoking cigarettes and drinking beer. Ulysses and Victor were there too. There were more girls, many girls, and a shining ball hung from the ceiling shooting out bright needles in all directions. Now he remembered sounds: a raucous music of

Moroccan violins and drums, whose purpose seemed to be to drown out the shrieks and arguments of the women.

"Nadia."

"Aisha."

Kisses on both cheeks. Repeated orders of drinks and cigarettes. A misunderstanding? One girl had pointed to the other with her finger and shouted:

"Syphilis!"

A fight.

Another place, very similar to the first.

A trip in two taxis—he and his two friends and three women were driven to a hotel on the outskirts. At the front desk, a receptionist with the look of a cop demanded money and passports.

"The passport!" he moaned between his teeth. He rolled out of bed and went to get his jacket and pants from the back of a chair—they stank of smoke. He rummaged among the disordered clothes of his suitcase, all the while remembering, with equal parts regret and frustration, the scene from last night: Ulysses and Victor walking toward the elevator with their girls; his own girl, irritated, watching him search uselessly through his pockets; the receptionist fixing him with a look of Muslim disdain.

It was Friday. From a nearby mosque, a muezzin called the mid-day prayer. While good Muslims bowed on their rugs to pray, he took a shower long enough to use up the hot water supply of the hotel. Then, wrapped in a large white towel, he fell back on the bed. He lifted up the phone and asked the operator the number of the Colombian consulate. He dialed it, but no one answered.

He got dressed and went down to the reception desk. He wrote down the particulars of the consulate and asked the receptionist how to get there.

"That's in the Casbah," he said. "But today's Friday and it's late." He looked at his watch. "I don't think they'll see you."

"I need to send a fax."

"You can do that here, but it's expensive. Better to do it from a teleboutique. There are plenty of them nearby."

He left the hotel, thinking the receptionist's good advice was due more to laziness than honesty. Musa Ben Nusair Street was deserted. Fridays in Morocco were special days. People crowded into the mosques to listen to the sermons of the imams; he'd been told their attacks on the government and the Sultan's family were increasingly explicit. And meanwhile his friends were probably fornicating. What mixture of pleasure and disgust would they experience, he wondered. Turning down a street formerly called Velázquez but that now had an Arab name, he walked toward the Faro internet café, which he knew from an earlier visit. He started to compose in his mind the message he would send home; he felt irritated that he'd have to lie but relieved that now he had a valid excuse for putting off his return.

XI

Victor and Ulysses looked like new, freshly bathed, as they sat drinking whiskey in their room.

"So what happened, *che boludo*?" Ulysses said, putting on an Argentine accent. "Did you find the passport?"

"No," he said, collapsing on the sofa. Victor handed him a glass of whiskey.

"Well, then?" asked Ulysses.

"I'm staying," he said with a smile. "How did it go last night?"

Victor shrugged and lifted his hands. "So-so."

"For me," said Ulysses, "phenomenal!"

"Whoremonger," Victor sneered.

"What can I say? The thing is to get off. Anyway, they're not really whores—not like ours, I mean. There's a big difference."

"Uh-huh. And what's that?" he asked.

It wasn't a question likely to leave Ulysses indifferent. He started to pace back and forth across the room. If, as their old philosophy professor used to argue, marriage and prostitution were two sides of the coin of respectable society, it was logical that a polygamous society would engender a different kind of prostitute. Which type was less sad? he asked.

"The question of legality aside," he continued, "if you're getting services like this for a certain amount of money, you have to ask to what extent you can be unbiased. Lots of girls here prostitute themselves to build up a dowry, without which they can't hope to get married. Later they marry and become respectable women. Put yourself in the place of a Moroccan girl. Suppose she's pretty and she's poor? What do you expect?"

"Balls, Ulysses. You're getting sentimental," said Victor. "Besides, the dowry thing here is the other way round. It's the groom that has to pay."

Ulysses stretched out on his back on the bed.

"Really? Anyway, this girl—Nadia—was sweet as can be."

"You're going to see her again?"

Ulysses sat up again.

"Probably not. We fly out tomorrow morning. And you," he asked, "what are you going to do?"

"Stay here, what else? And wait. Can't you see her before you go?"

"No, she'll be sleeping. They start work at midnight and sleep all day. The night-time schedule keeps them out of circulation, so they don't mingle with 'decent' folks in the daylight."

"Well," said Victor, "what did she do for you?"

Ulysses closed his eyes with a smile of pleasure.

"Everything I wanted, she knew."

"Why don't you give your passport to this guy who's got a wife in Cali waiting for him, and you could stay here?"

Ulysses thought about it a moment and said:

"I would, I really would. If I didn't have to work."

XII

He turned up Velázquez Street toward Boulevard Pasteur and the Faro Plaza, where there were only a few people—some shoeshine boys and photographers hanging around the Portuguese cannon. The metal blinds of the stores were shut. Some early swallows circled the tops of the oaks in the garden of the French consulate. Leaving his route to chance, he turned at Rue de la Liberté, so as to head back down to the Zoco de Fuera. Passing the Hotel Minzah, he stopped and looked into a shop window filled with dusty Berber daggers, bracelets, and necklaces. Then he kept going. He crossed the cement plaza of the old Zoco and entered the Medina by the south gate. He turned down toward the Zoco Chico by Plateros Street, where there were more people. A vendor poured water from a goat skin into zinc cups. The girls—some veiled, some not—shot curious glances. Just like the girls in Cali, he thought. In the middle of the rectangular plaza he stopped, and a slender, pale Moroccan with a week's beard came up to ask him what he was looking for. Without answering, he looked around him, then sat down at a little table on the café terrace. It was on the upper part of the plaza, where the sun hit.

From the back of the café came wisps of Egyptian music and the noise of a television. A mix of odors floated out too: oranges, mint, burned grease, and, for an instant, the smell of kif. He breathed deeply, feeling the desire to smoke. He raised his hand to call the waiter and ordered a Coca-Cola.

In front of him, Moroccan heads passed by, then seemed to

multiply. The mosques would be emptying out, he thought. Eyes that reminded him of other eyes, but in different faces. A familiar nose beneath an unexpected forehead, too narrow— features brought together by chance as in a book of sketches by a prolific and careless artist.

After a while, a poor-looking Moroccan walked up to the terrace and sat at the next table. He turned to look at him and said in Spanish:

"Excuse me, don't we know each other?"

"I don't think so."

"Spanish?"

"No," he answered, turning back to look at the plaza.

"You look like a friend of mine."

From where he sat, he could still see the Moroccan who had approached him in the plaza; he was leaning against a wooden case where he had spread out contraband packs of cigarettes. Before the waiter arrived, he watched the man make a deal with a long-haired tourist brought to him by a street boy. The man exchanged a few words with his customer in the middle of the plaza and led him toward a narrow intersection where they made the transaction.

He said in a lowered voice to the Muslim:

"That guy, the one with the cigarettes, what's he selling?"

"Drugs."

"What kind of drugs?"

"All kinds. Hashish, cocaine, pills. Everything."

"Kif?"

The other laughed.

"I doubt if he sells kif. Only old men smoke kif. Where are you from?"

"Colombia."

"Ah," said the Muslim, "the Colombian mafia."

"That's right."

The other put out his hand, which he couldn't refuse.

"Glad to meet you, my friend." A vigorous handshake. "My name is Rashid." A few seconds later: "Tourist?"

"Not exactly."

"Business?"

"Something like that."

"How long are you staying in Tangier?"

"I don't know."

"All right. You need something, anything, no problem—I'm always here."

"I'd like to get some kif," he said.

"Yes?"

"Is it dangerous?"

"Dangerous? Kif? Bah. I don't smoke. You have to cut it, you know. But I can get you some. How much do you want?"

"Fifty dirhams?"

"No problem. Give me fifty dirhams."

"What?"

"You want kif, give me fifty dirhams."

"And when will I get it?"

"Tomorrow. At this time."

They stayed a little while longer in silence until he stood up. He laid a fifty-dirham bill on the table in front of Rashid and said:

"All right. I'll see you tomorrow."

XIII

Now the little shops were open. Tourist bazaars, leather stores, tiny jewelry shops that gleamed with golden objects. The day's lost now, he thought. Before leaving the Medina, he decided to amuse himself walking through the little streets, dark like tunnels, that rose and fell between dwarf houses and businesses spilling neon light, where odors and children alike moved freely from house to house. He went down a flight of urinous stairs that flanked the city wall and came out at last onto a wide straight street, the old Rue d'Italie, which sloped between two rows of trees and shops. Heaps of wool, towers of bowls, plastic flowers, straw mats, barber posts, bunches of shoes that hung like fruit from awnings or small balconies. A theater from which he could hear the rumble of a war movie. The smell of mint tea and tobacco floating on the café terraces. He stopped in front of an herbalist's display window. He went inside and saw porcupine and snake skins hanging from the walls, and a falcon—eye sockets vacant—grotesquely stuffed and mounted.

"What's it for?"

"To make fumes for healing," said the herbalist, who seemed to be a bit of a charlatan.

He left and continued walking uphill toward the Zoco de Fuera, along the fence that enclosed the Mendubía gardens, where with a huge ruckus thousands of swallows swirled above in the treetops.

XIV

He practically leapt down the stairs to Rue d'Italie—half-elated, half-outraged at the news from the honorary consul, who had told him it would be several weeks before he got his passport.

The Colombian consulate was nothing but a little apartment on top of the fortified arch of the Casbah gate. A small library, doubling as a waiting room, offered a view of the port, the bay, and the luminous Medina. From the consul's office, which gave onto a little elevated garden with roman cypresses and rose-bushes, one could see a large part of the new city, the camel-colored hills that surrounded it, and, much farther off, the foothills of the Rif. The consul had never been to Colombia, he said, and had no intention of going. He was a North American shipwrecked here by chance. This no longer mattered to him, he said, although the city was not even a shadow of what it had been when he first came. According to him, the mental evolution of the Moroccans was going in reverse. "Bad stock," he said. "The French knew it very well. They're good for only one thing," and he covered his mouth with one hand to emphasize the indiscretion.

If he bothered to keep the plaque on the door and to read and answer official letters, it was only because the title agreed with him, and he didn't mind receiving a visit from time to time.

"Especially from a nice-looking, civilized person like yourself," he added, to make his inclinations obvious. "So let's hope you enjoy your life here. Come to see me when you like." The consul held out a damp hand.

At the end of the street, on the sidewalk across from the herbalist's, he saw a ragged boy with a two-handled basket trying to sell a barn owl.

He stopped and leaned over the basket to examine it. The owl said *"chi chichich."* Its big black eyes, circled with ochre disks, looked straight ahead. Its old woman's face was framed by a halo of small feathers. It moved its head constantly, following the slightest movement around it.

"Can I touch it?" he asked, thinking the boy wouldn't understand.

"Touch it, touch it," the boy said.

He put out his hand and touched its head. The owl shut its eyes, as if in resignation. "Chi, chichich." He touched the tawny wings, with their thick, soft plumage, and noted the tear-shaped stains that adorned its back. He straightened up and looked at the boy.

"How much?" he asked.

"Mía dirham," the boy said.

"I don't understand."

"Cento, cento."

He smiled.

"Here's fifty." He counted to fifty with both hands, as children do.

The boy stared a moment at the herbalist's shop, scratched his head, and finally, putting out his dirty, eager hand, said:

"*Ara hamsín.*"

The boy pocketed the money and lifted up the owl, whose well-feathered legs were tied with a piece of rope. The man took it in both hands. He said, "Easy now, precious," adjusting it against his chest and holding it firmly. He set out up the street, now crowded with people and suddenly seeming much noisier than ever.

XV

In his room at the Atlas, he untied the owl's feet and set it on a little dressing table. It fluttered its wings listlessly. Then it hopped up and perched on the back of an armchair; fastening its claws, it shook its head once and fixed its large eyes on its new owner. "To inspect me," he thought to himself. It spread its wide, rounded wings and produced the sound "*kiúk*," twice. He crossed the room, from the dressing table toward the balcony door, the owl following him with its eyes, turning its head. He drew the curtains, and the owl blinked. When he sat down on the bed, the owl's eyes followed him with another revolution of its head and remained fixed on him. He took off his shoes to lie back and sleep; the owl observed his movements with tiny oscillations of its head.

He woke up with a slight weight on one shoulder, his face buried in the down pillow. He turned slowly and saw the owl's face, examining him with almost human curiosity. "Hello, beautiful," he said. He lay face up, and the bird leaped and perched on his hip. It opened its white, arched beak, closed it, and opened it again. "Yes, precious, we're going to look for something for you to eat." He shifted, and the owl flew over and perched on the back of the armchair again. He put his shoes on quickly and stood up. "I'll be right back," he said.

It was almost midnight. The doorman, sleeping in an easy chair in the lobby, got up with a jerk and drew back the bolt of the door to let him out.

"*M'salkheir*," he said.

At this time of night, the city seemed less Mediterranean than Asian, with its food stalls and stores flooded with sickly neon light. The street smelled of diesel and burned meat. The cats, almost invisible by day in this part of the city, where they were harassed by the Moroccans, took over the sidewalks by night and were left alone ("because nobody in his right mind would ever strike a cat in darkness").

"Become who you really are," said a display for Lacoste in a window on the Boulevard Pasteur. On the other side, a glowing Wimpy's sign shone on the sidewalk. He crossed the street, the empty taxis cruising slowly, and went into a small Muslim diner.

"*Kefta?*" he asked, looking at the display window, where there were two large pewter plates each bearing a mound of ground beef, surrounded by cans of *Jus d'or* and Fanta, each can topped with a red tomato.

"Spanish?"

"Yes. Some ground beef. Raw, please."

"How much?"

"Half a kilo."

The Moroccan took a piece of red meat, weighed it on a marble table, and cut it into several pieces, which he inserted into the grinder. Then he wrapped the mass in a sheet of paper, put it into a plastic bag, and set it on the imitation marble counter.

"*Báraca l-láh u fik.*"

"*B'saha.*"

Back in the hotel, he opened the package on the dressing

table, and saw with dismay that bits of coriander or parsley had been mixed in with the meat. He took a bit of meat in his fingers, made a little ball, rolling it on the palm of his hand, and approached the owl. It had left the back of the chair to perch on one of the tin wall-lamps at the head of the bed.

"All right," he said, shooing it, "get down from there. It's time to eat."

The owl flew back to the armchair. When he drew close with the meat, it opened its beak greedily and swallowed the meat with no difficulty. It opened its beak again, asking for more.

"Well, then," he said to the owl, after it had devoured almost all of the meat, "now it's my turn." He went to the bathroom to wash his hands, then headed for the street in search of a restaurant.

When he returned, the owl was again perched on the wall-lamp over the bed. There was a greenish white puddle on one of the pillows.

"Oh, no." He threw up his arms in anger. "Get out of there!"

The owl opened its beak and spread its wings defiantly. Then it flew back to the armchair, raised its short tail, and let fall a stream of greenish liquid onto the Berber rug.

"Oh, this is a great start."

He rolled up his sleeves and began to pull off the pillow-cases.

The owl hooted.

XVI

Leaving the room in disorder—the pillowcase balled up in a corner, the half-washed rug spread out on the balcony—and the owl locked up in the bathroom, he went out for breakfast. On the broad white terrace of the Café Ziryab with its little plastic tables—from which he could see in the distance the Djebel Musa, the pale pillar of Hercules collapsed on the African shore—the sun had flooded everything in orange light. He took off his sunglasses and sat contemplating the scene—a white boat moved off toward Gibraltar, leaving a wide, creamy wake. For the moment, he was satisfied and happy.

Before going back to the hotel, he walked down to the Zoco de Fuera, which was bustling with activity. At the market entrance, women from the country in wide-brimmed hats were selling fresh cottage cheese and big loaves of bread. Inside the market, he could smell flowers, milk, and fresh meat. He approached a butcher's stand and asked for chicken guts; he watched a man with a long knife at the neighboring stand strip all the meat but the eyes from a goat's head. Farther on, in front of a flower stand, someone was selling birdcages. He decided a cage was a good idea.

He was waiting for the elevator in the Atlas, which came down humming amid clangs of chains and gears, when the porter, Abdelkhay, gave him two vigorous slaps—too vigorous, he thought—on the shoulder.

Abdelkhay smiled, but it was not a friendly smile.

"Señor," he said, "no animals. You have an animal. You have to go. Understand?"

"How's that?"

Now the Muslim seemed agitated.

"You have to go!" he shouted.

"Why?" He opened the elevator door.

"The boss told me to tell you. That's all."

"Really? Where is your boss?"

"He's not here. But the bird cannot stay."

"All right," he said, stepping into the elevator. "I'll go."

The car started to rise. Abdelkhay, who kept on looking at him through the grille, shouted, "Bad bird! Bad bird!" before his face disappeared under the elevator floor.

XVII

The bed was unmade; they had taken the sheets and pillowcases. The Berber rug had disappeared, and the curtains on the glass door were open wide. Three or four pigeons walked on the balcony railing. He closed the glass door and went to the bathroom, where he found the owl perched on the edge of the tub. It opened its beak and unfurled its wings. "Yes, get out of here, there's too much light in this room." It flew close by him, expertly, into the bedroom and landed on the dressing table. It looked at itself in the mirror. Then it turned its head around and looked at him, still standing beside the door. "We're going to move, girl. The trouble is I don't know where yet." He went back to the bathroom to wash his hands.

"Fuck!" he yelled. They had taken all the towels.

Drying his hands on his pants and in his hair, he went back to the bedroom and sat on the bed. He looked at the telephone. He ought to tell the consulate he was moving out of the hotel.

XVIII

The honorary consul acted as if he were used to situations like this.

"An owl—I see. That's interesting. Come in, come in. Leave it there. That's fine. And what are you doing with an owl?"

He left his bag behind the parlor door and set the cage on a Moroccan chest. Someone shouted something in Arabic in another apartment and a door closed.

"That's Morad," explained the consul, "my friend from Rabat. Won't you sit down? What happened at the Atlas?"

"It messed all over the place."

"They are certainly right, the hotel people. This is not a bird they're going to like, no sir," he said, rolling his eyes. "And what do you plan to do?"

"Look for another hotel, to start with. I'll let the bird go, naturally. But it seems a bit young. And I think it's weak."

The consul gazed at him. He was not interested in the owl but in him.

"What can I do for you?"

"Can I leave my things here while I look for another room?"

"Where will you look?"

"I'm thinking of a pension in the Medina. I don't think they'll object."

The consul's face changed. The idea of staying in a pension in the Medina was unthinkable.

"If you can live in places like that . . . But then you can, of course, you're young." He paused. "Listen," he said, "you wouldn't be selling drugs, would you?"

"No. Of course not."

"Fine. Anyway, you can be frank with me."

"I guess I'd better be going. You don't know how grateful I am." He stood up and leaned over the cage, looking at the owl. "Goodbye, precious," he said. "You'll be safe here."

"Precious, eh?" the consul repeated mockingly. "You're as crazy as everyone else in this blessed country."

The consul walked with him to the stairs, which descended directly to the street door. Before closing it behind him, he heard the consul saying:

"Morad! Come see what our new Colombian friend brought us."

XIX

The sun was blazing high in the magnificent Moroccan sky, but down among the dim and narrow streets it was damp and cold. He walked quickly through a sloping labyrinth, where now and again he could smell the sea. In the wider parts, vendors stood pressed against the walls, selling crockery, natural cosmetics, vegetables, and fish. Finally he came to the Zoco Chico, where, in the Café Tingis, Rashid sat at a little table with two other men, filling out football betting cards. He sat down a few feet away.

"Hercules, Toledo . . ." one of the men recited, while the others said "1," "x," or "2."

"Numancia, Compostela . . . Mallorca, Atlético de Madrid . . ."

When they were finished, Rashid excused himself and came to sit with him.

"What's new, my friend? I don't have your kif yet."

"I didn't come for that. I'm looking for a pension."

"You want to live in a pension? Around here?"

"Why not?"

"No . . . nothing." Rashid looked at his hands for a moment. "I know two or three. If you want, I'll take you."

"The problem is that I have an owl."

"Ah, yes, an owl?" He smiled. "You have an owl?" He seemed amused.

"I'm told that people around here don't like them. In Colombia a lot of people think they bring bad luck."

"Why? There are stupid people everywhere. It's just a bird. I don't believe in that foolishness. Good luck or bad luck—I'm a good Muslim; I can't believe in nonsense."

"You'll help me find a pension?"

"Yes, of course. *Yal-lah.*"

They got up.

XX

They headed down the old Rue de la Poste, where they met a poor young woman dressed in a ragged military uniform. Rashid explained that her husband had been captured by the Algerians, or by the Polisario, when he was serving in the army. She thought he was still alive, and had been saving money for over ten years to travel south to look for him, Rashid said.

"Here it is."

"Pension Calpe," said the sign painted in red ink on an iron door. The tiled hallway smelled of dirty feet and lye, and the walls were covered in grime. A fat Moroccan, dressed in a frayed djellaba and plastic slippers, showed them a room on the second floor. It was larger than he had expected. The semidarkness was convenient; only one small window, which looked onto a narrow inner patio, let in the daylight. A naked bulb hung from the ceiling. Though the bed was very narrow, the sheets looked clean.

"Will it do?" asked Rashid.

"Yes, it's fine."

"Pay him."

"What?"

"If you want the room, you pay the man now."

"All right," he said. "I'll be back this afternoon."

They went out to the street.

"Now," said Rashid, "you can buy me a coffee."

XXI

He followed Rashid uphill along a little street that smelled of sewage and dead bodies. They were going to a little smokers' café, Rashid said, where they could find a kif cutter.

"The other day, I was talking to two kids who make money catching dogs," Rashid said. "They use them to fool the dogs at the Spanish customs. They sell them to a truck driver who smuggles hashish in his truck. He cuts a dog's throat and sprinkles its blood where the shit is stashed. They say that as soon as the police dogs catch a whiff of the blood, they back off; the smell scares them."

"Incredible."

"How could I make up something like that?"

"And it works?"

"I guess. What do I know?"

They came to the café, a dark cubicle with four little tables along a wall grotesquely painted with a desert scene—dunes, a camel, and palm trees. The tea maker, an old man with a turban and vest, greeted Rashid and gave the newcomer a look of indifference or distrust.

They sat down on a straw mattress with their backs against the wall. The old man served them tea and then eased himself down onto a small wooden platform covered with a rattan mat beside another Moroccan, a young man with long hair and large dirty yellow teeth who was busy cutting kif on a wooden plank. The smell of the herb mixed pleasantly with that of mint and orange blossom.

"*Bismil-láh,*" said Rashid and took a sip of tea.

The crazy young woman in uniform popped her head in from the street to ask for money.

"Give her something," Rashid suggested. He obeyed, taking a five-dirham coin from his pocket and dropping it in her outstretched hand.

"*Báraca l-láh u fik,*" she said, and with a bow to Rashid, left the café.

Rashid smiled with satisfaction.

"That's good," he said. "She's a good woman."

Half an hour later, he left the café with a ball of kif bulging in his pocket. On the way to the pension, he stopped at a stand to buy some cigarettes; he asked for the cheapest brand.

XXII

The honorary consul's gardener opened the door for him and pointed the way up the stairs to the waiting room. The suitcase was behind the door, where he had left it, but the cage was no longer on the chest. From the dining room, accessible by a little spiral staircase, came the smell of coffee and the voices of the consul and Morad, the friend from Rabat, having an after-dinner talk. They were speaking English.

"He's certainly not bad. I already told you I was interested in him," said the consul. "Very interested. You've seen him, haven't you?"

"Does he have any money?"

"How would I know? It's not his money that interests me."

The other laughed.

"Well, then, what?"

"I know where you're going with this. Don't worry. He just seems like someone with whom one can have a conversation. That's important to me."

"A conversation about what? Owls?" The Moroccan laughed. "What do you know about why he's here? He wouldn't tell you if it's what I think. How much do you think it'll cost?"

Hearing all this, he was confused and wondered whether to go up to the dining room or to stay where he was. But he heard the noise of chairs moving and decided to go back down the flight of stairs toward the front door. He started down slowly. Then he heard steps coming down the spiral staircase. So he turned and walked up again, decisively, toward the waiting room.

"*Hombre,* so you're here," said the consul, giving him his hand.

Morad looked to be twenty years old; he was dressed in European clothes with considerable style. The consul introduced them.

"Where's the owl?" he asked, as nicely as he could.

"In the garden. Don't worry. We put a blanket over it. Yes. They hate the daylight."

"What are you going to do with it?" asked Morad with an Andalusian lilt.

"Let it go, I suppose."

"Let it go? No, you should give it to me," Morad said.

The consul smiled.

"Come, come," he said. "Nothing will happen to it. Look, I'll explain. Morad has fallen in love with the owl. He adores it. He wants it to be his. Do you understand? And he's prepared to pay for it. How much is it worth?"

"It's not for sale."

"But he's very interested."

"Really?" He smiled. "How much could he pay?"

The consul turned to Morad.

"It's for my uncle that I want it. He has a collection of birds. He has several owls, with and without ears. He'd like this one, I'm sure. I could give you as much as a thousand—dirhams, I mean, certainly not dollars!"

He thought a moment, then shook his head.

"Thanks very much," he added a second later.

The Moroccan touched himself at the pit of his stomach. Then he moved his hand vaguely and managed to say politely:

"It's an honest offer."

"I don't say it isn't," he replied. Now he could permit himself the luxury of being affable. "But I don't like the idea of this owl being part of some collection."

"Ah, I understand," said the Moroccan. There was something faintly menacing in his voice. "It's because of that."

"One can always change one's mind," said the consul, trying to be diplomatic.

Morad smiled, but the smile did not add up to a smile.

"Have you found lodging?" asked the consul.

"Yes, I was lucky."

"Splendid. And now I suppose you want your bird, eh?" He leaned his head toward the stairs and shouted, "Mohammed! Mohammed! The gentleman's bird."

XXIII

With the weight of the suitcase on his shoulder and the caged owl in the other hand, he walked down Riad Sultán Street alongside the wall that bordered the Casbah on the ocean side. On the plaza of the Casbah, under the walls of the old prison, a group of Spanish tourists had gathered. A guide wearing a white djellaba and a fez was telling them about King Alfonso VI, who had given Tangier as his sister Catarina's dowry to Charles II of England. Several begging children circled among the tourists, kissing their hands, their sleeves, and the folds of their shirts.

He entered the Medina by the Bab el Bahr, the seaside gate, and turned onto a downgrade lane toward Ben Rasuli Street, where a boy with a shaved head began to run beside him. The boy stuck out his hand to ask for money. "No," he said. "No, not now." "Give me dirham. Poor. Poor. To eat." He made a gesture as if to put something in his mouth and then he grabbed his sleeve and brought his lips close to it. "No!" But the boy held onto his shirt with an unexpected strength, and even though he gave a sharp tug to free himself, he couldn't. "Let go, now!" he shouted. At that moment another Moroccan boy, older than the first, came up on his right and, giving him a shove, seized the cage and began to run with it downhill.

"Hey! Stop! Thief!" he shouted, and, striking the first boy, got free of him and started running after the thief.

He didn't know the little streets, but he could hear the sound of the thief's footsteps.

Once he made a wrong turn up a dead-end street, but an old man fixing a tin teapot in the recess of a wall pointed the way to him, and, doubling back, he was just able to see the thief turning a corner a few yards down the labyrinth. The owl's cage banged a wall leaving a groove in the stucco. I'll never catch him carrying this suitcase, he thought. He came out into a long sloping street and saw the thief running hard a few meters below. He stopped, breathless and now resigned, telling himself that Morad couldn't have had time to send the boy to steal the bird, when he saw that, at the bottom of the street, turning sharply to go up a side path, the thief had slipped and fallen hard on his back, his legs in the air. The owl's cage had flown up in the air and fallen in front of the door of a carpet vendor, who stuck his head out to see what was happening. He yelled again: "Hey! Thief! That man's a thief!" and ran down the street. The thief got up quickly and disappeared, leaving the cage where it landed, a few steps from the skid marks.

XXIV

Attup, the bear-like Muslim who worked as receptionist at the Pension Calpe, raised no objection to the owl, but he wanted to see a passport. An ATM card and a Colombian driver's license satisfied him for the moment. Attup spoke almost no Spanish, but with gestures and a few French words, he let him know it was not a good idea to be without a passport. Lately, he explained, the gendarmes had been making raids on the little hotels of the Medina, rounding up undocumented aliens—mostly Africans from Mali or Senegal who came to Tangier in the hope of getting to Europe, crossing the straits of Gibraltar. The police could give him problems, Attup said. He should pay a visit to the commissariat, where they would give him a temporary identity card.

"Thanks very much. I'll do it right away."

"*Joli oiseau*," said Attup. "*Vraiment joli.*"

Attup accompanied him to his room on the second floor and gave him his key. He laid the suitcase on the bed and set the cage at the foot of an old radiator under the window. He followed Attup down the stairs to the table by the staircase, which served as reception desk, and asked him where he could find the nearest commissariat. In the new sector, said Attup. He advised him to take some photos also, as they would be necessary. He pointed out a photographer's studio not far from the pension.

"If I had the power," he told him, "I would make *you* the honorary consul of Colombia."

Attup smiled faintly.

"*B'slama*," he said.

"See you later."

XXV

Photos taken, temporary identification arranged with the police, chicken guts purchased for the bird, he went back in the afternoon to the pension. The owl was asleep in its cage. He was tired, and his face was covered with grease and exhaust—it was just like walking the streets of Cali, he thought. He took his toilet things from the suitcase, put on some plastic slippers, and went out in search of the bathroom, which, as a sign in French indicated, stood at the end of the hallway on the other side of a small patio. The tiles, covered with a greenish film, were dangerously slippery, and the barely lukewarm water fell lazily from a rusted pipe. It was possible to wash up: the thing was not to let any part of your body come in contact with the walls and not to let the bar of soap fall on the floor.

Back in the room, after getting dressed, he opened the little door of the cage to let the owl out. It was still growing, he thought, seeing it hop up to perch on the radiator. He noticed that its left wing had slightly fallen, but he wasn't worried. He unwrapped the loosely packed bundle of entrails while he kept his eye on the owl, which stared back at him and opened its beak.

He threw a piece of chicken liver at its feet and it jumped to the floor.

"What happened to your wing?" he asked, seeing the owl was dragging it. He drew near, took the wing softly by its point, and extended it. The owl, with a sudden jerk, pecked him hard on the knuckle.

"Hey!" He drew back, surprised, but he knew it was a reflex: its wing was hurt. There was a blood stain on the feathers near the joint. He took a step back and sat down on the edge of the bed.

XXVI

Wrapped in a cloud of kif smoke, seated in a lotus position on his bed in the pension, his back against the cold, damp wall, he invented a Moroccan future for himself. He wouldn't go home for a long time. He'd learn Arabic. Maybe he'd become a Muslim. He'd buy a Berber wife. He had been alone a long time, after all. How many weeks had it been since he came to Tangier?

All at once he felt hungry. After counting his money and seeing with alarm how little was left—a hundred and twenty dirhams—he took his bank card and left the pension toward Boulevard Pasteur, where he knew there were teller machines.

He tried to withdraw money several times, from three different ATMs, but had no luck. His wife hadn't made the deposit he'd asked her to make. This was a tight spot, but he wasn't going to panic. He turned his back on the last ATM and set out for the Place de France.

The young woman in the ragged uniform was begging among the tables on the terrace of the Café de Paris. When he walked by her, she stopped begging and watched him. He smiled and she put out her hand. Without thinking, he put his hand in his pocket where he had a twenty-dirham bill, and, with a recklessness that surprised him, gave it to her.

"God be with you," she said. She pressed the bill to her lips and walked off, crossing the plaza toward Fez Street.

He turned up another street, suddenly full of conflicting energies, happy at his own unforeseen generosity but confused, even alarmed, at the insecurity of his situation. "It must be the kif," he thought.

It was just a matter of time until one of the ATMs would function, but the fact of being without money had an almost physical effect on him. He felt light. Now he walked very fast, uphill or downhill.

XXVII

"This is nothing," said Rashid. "My friend will cure it."

He put the owl in the cage.

"Your friend—what kinds of animals does he cure?"

"Mostly cattle and sheep, but sometimes people take dogs and cats to him."

"I wonder if he knows about birds."

"He's bound to know something. They take chickens to him too."

The veterinarian's office was out in Achakar, a small plateau overlooking the Atlantic, south of Cape Spartel. It was a square house, surrounded by a vegetable garden with a pergola and a well.

A dog sprang out of a tipped-over oil drum and started to bark, yanking the rope that held it. The wind was blowing and some dry thistles scratched against the rusted side of the drum and made it squeak. Telling Rashid he would wait for them there, the taxi driver got out of his broken-down Mercedes and walked over to look at some camel tracks in the dry, sandy earth by the roadside.

Doctor Al Rudani was seated behind a white desk in a parlor with green walls and a gray floor. He was tall, dark, big-nosed, and his smock was neatly pressed. The place smelled of chloroform and ammonia.

"Let's have a look," he said. "What have you got there, Rashid?"

Rashid spoke in Arabic with the doctor. Then the doctor turned to him, greeted him in Spanish, and asked about the situation in Colombia. He leaned over to look at the owl.

"May I?"

He took the cage, set it on a metal table, and put on latex gloves. He turned on a powerful lamp and, carefully but firmly, took the owl out of the cage. Holding its head with one hand, he pulled open the wounded wing with the other. The owl turned around sharply, stretching out its claws and flapping its good wing, then fell completely still. The doctor did not seem to like what he saw. He cleaned a bit of blood with a ball of cotton. "Tch, tch." He lifted up two feathers between his fingers and released them; they fell slowly back in place.

"Poor thing," said the doctor. "I don't think she'll fly again."

Without releasing the owl's head, he held it by the legs and put it back into the cage.

He turned off the lamp. "There's nothing I can do."

"You mean there's no cure?"

"I'm afraid not. If you like, you can leave it with me—I'll put her to sleep."

"To sleep?" he asked.

"Yes. You know, the big sleep." The doctor smiled.

"No, by no means."

Rashid shrugged his shoulders, as if excusing himself.

"You should have sold it," he said. "Now it's worthless."

He took the cage.

"Thank you, doctor."

"It won't fly again," the doctor repeated. "It will suffer a lot, that's all."

He lifted the cage and looked at the owl, which seemed startled.

"I hope you're wrong. But thanks anyway."

At this moment two women entered the clinic. The older woman, about fifty, cradled a black Pekingese, which appeared to be either dead or unconscious, in her arms. She walked straight up to the doctor. The other, twenty years younger, waited by the door.

"Ah, Mme. Choiseul," exclaimed the doctor, who promptly left Rashid to take the Pekingese.

"Look at it, would you?" the woman said in French.

The doctor set the little dog on the metal table. He turned on the lamp again and with two fingers opened one of the dog's eyes.

"Let's see now." He began to examine the dog, touching its abdomen, while Mme. Choiseul caressed its head maternally.

The younger woman stared at the owl. She gave its owner a smile and said in French:

"Pretty bird."

"Thank you."

"Is it yours?"

"Yes."

She drew near. Although she was slightly cross-eyed, he found her attractive.

"Did something happen to it?"

"The doctor thinks it's got a broken wing," he answered in French.

"Oh, what a pity."

"Yes, he says there's nothing he can do."

"Look at those eyes! How did it get hurt?"

"It's a long story."

Rashid stood in the doorway. "Shall we go?" he said. "The taxi is waiting."

"Yes, just a moment," he answered.

"I'll wait outside."

The woman smiled.

"Where are you going?"

"To Tangier."

"Is he your friend?"

"Not really. He's sort of a guide."

"We're going to Tangier too. We could give you a ride." She hesitated. "You don't mind that I speak to you as *tu*?"

"No, of course not. Thank you."

"If you like, I'll hold the bird, no?"

He gave her the cage.

"Sure," he said.

He came out of the clinic into the late afternoon light. Rashid and the taxi driver sat in the Mercedes. He leaned his head toward the window and said to Rashid:

"These ladies are going to take me."

"All right. But pay the driver."

He took his last fifty dirhams out of his wallet and gave them to Rashid.

"That's not enough."

"Rashid, I don't have any more." He opened his wallet to show him.

"The price is one hundred," said the driver to Rashid, "and that's because it's you."

"I'll pay you later, Rashid."

"Give me a guarantee," Rashid said, irritated.

"All right." He took off his wristwatch and handed it to him. Rashid smiled.

"That's good." He turned to the driver. "Let's go. I'll pay you in the Medina," he said in Arabic.

The wheels of the Mercedes shot out gravel and raised two little clouds of dust. The doctor's dog did not stop barking until the car had swung onto the asphalt road to silhouette itself against the sky and the sea. Then it crawled back into its barrel.

XXVIII

Inside the clinic, the little Pekingese had come to. It stood up on the table, wagging its tail. It barked twice hoarsely, gave a little jump, breathed hard, and shook its head.

"What an actor," said Mme. Choiseul. "He just wanted us to take him for a ride in the car." She turned to her friend. "Right, Julie? I assure you, doctor, he's faking these fainting spells."

"I don't think so," said the doctor. "But only Allah knows all."

The woman picked the dog up and put it on the floor, where it barked and ran circles around her.

"All right, Taubin, shut up." She opened her purse to take out a hundred-dirham note, which she gave to the doctor.

"Thank you," he said. "Until next time."

"Ah, what heavenly light," said Mme. Choiseul as she stepped into the evening breeze. The Pekingese ran over to urinate against a row of sand-colored rocks that bordered the doctor's garden, then turned to inspect the strange camel prints in the middle of the road. The doctor's dog silently crept out of its barrel and hurled itself at the Pekingese, which saw it only at the last instant. It jerked its body sideways and yelped.

"Oh, the poor bird," exclaimed Mme. Choiseul, looking at the owl. "It should be free."

The sun hadn't set, but the heat of the day was gone.

"Let's go," said the younger woman. "I'm cold. Maybe the gentleman can explain to us on the way what he's doing with an owl."

They got into the car. The little dog, showing no interest in the owl, barked at some children selling pine nuts by the roadside. The eucalypti and mimosas parted on either side of the car, their odor pouring in through the windows.

"I'm here by accident," he began to explain.

After giving a somewhat glamorized version of his story, he learned that Julie Bachelier was a student of archaeology, interested in the Roman and pre-Roman history of the area. She was on vacation, staying at Mme. Choiseul's house on the outskirts of Tangier. Mme. Choiseul's first name was Christine. She was an exceptionally bad driver.

For a moment, he imagined the two women embracing each other.

"My mother is an accountant," said Julie. "She works for Christine in Paris."

He decided he was interested in Julie.

"You have a Moroccan face," Mme. Choiseul told him.

"So I've been told," he replied. "I don't think I'd like to be Moroccan."

"Do you like being Colombian?"

"To tell the truth, not much. No."

The Frenchwomen agreed: it would be better to have been born European.

"But in Europe I feel suffocated. Too much organization," he said.

From the heights of R'milat one could see the city of Tangier lying in the hills, like a wide salt marsh in the evening light. Passing the giant palaces of the Saudi princes, Mme. Choiseul turned on a narrow road that descended between two high stucco walls, now in disrepair and heaped with bougainvillea and honeysuckle in flower.

"Oh, what am I doing?" she shouted. "Where was it you were going? My mind was wandering—I was going to our house."

"To the Medina."

"The Medina? What are you going to do there?"

"I'm staying there, in a pension."

"Really?" said Julie.

"I haven't found anywhere else that will take me in with the bird. It's really a bit depressing."

"Well, then," said Julie, "you can't be in much of a hurry to go home. Why don't we invite him for coffee with us, Christine?"

"*Mais oui*," said Mme. Choiseul. Looking in the rearview mirror to see what he would say, she nearly scraped the right side of the car against a wall. "*Oh là là!*" she cried.

XXIX

Mme. Choiseul's house, in the upper reaches of the Sidi Mesmudi road, stood on a small plateau surrounded by a large olive garden, a high curtain of eucalypti, and a canebrake.

"Artifo!" she shouted, getting out of the car and letting loose the Pekingese, which ran toward the lower part of the yard.

The garden, descending in small terraces, had a fountain, many narrow flower beds, and, farther down, a black monkey tree that rose up against the sky.

Artifo, an old man with a close-cropped beard and a fisherman's cap, appeared in a side door.

"Yes, Madame?"

"Tell Fátima we're going to have tea. And light the fire in the living room and in my room. It has to be done every day," she explained, turning her back on Artifo.

They came out of the garage. From where they stood the sound of waves could be heard under the murmur of the wind in the branches. But the shore had to be far off, he thought.

They passed through a dark hall into a living room decorated with many potted plants and flowers where the dwindling light came through several small arched windows. The walls were upholstered in red, pink, and violet satin bands, and the floor was spongy, thick with Berber rugs covered with designs suggesting hands and eyes. The little coffee tables were stacked with art books, and the bookshelves were also heavy with old volumes. Julie took the birdcage from his hands and put it on a sideboard between two windows.

As they sat down next to the fireplace, Mme. Choiseul on a small sofa, with the Pekingese on her lap, Julie on a Moroccan pouf, her arms around her knees, and he on a low couch, Artifo covered a heap of dry eucalyptus leaves with sticks of firewood and lit them.

The colors of the room brightened with the first flames and a medicinal smell enveloped them.

"I know it's not so cold as to need a fire," said Mme. Choiseul, whose cheeks were turning red in the firelight, "but it's not too hot to light one either. I worship fire." She looked at the fireplace. "I get cold easily."

Artifo left the room.

Now Mme. Choiseul looked at the owl.

"It's lovely," she said, and turned toward him. "The Moroccans have a whole repertory of animal stories, did you know? There's one about an owl."

An old woman, slightly stooped, with a white kerchief tied around her head, appeared at the door from the kitchen, carrying a large tea service.

XXX

They sipped their tea and talked about trivialities: the situation of Morocco, the possibilities for change, the fate of Pinochet, and the similarities and differences between Pinochet and the Sultan.

"Obviously, everyone ought to be able to express himself about anything, but not on the radio or in the press. There are limits," Julie was saying.

Mme. Choiseul was more interested in learning how the owl had been injured than in discussing the limits of freedom in a Muslim nation.

He told the story of the thief in the Medina.

"Who would want to steal an owl?" Julie asked. "Are they valuable?"

"I know that they sometimes hunt them," said Mme. Choiseul. "They're easy to trap. I don't think they're worth a lot, but of course that is relative. Any little boy can catch one."

"And what do they use them for?" Julie wanted to know.

"God knows," said Mme. Choiseul, "but clearly they can sell them."

He told them then how the consul's friend had offered him a thousand dirhams for the bird.

"Maybe it was a joke," he said at last.

"But do you suspect him?"

"It seems absurd."

"The Honorary Consul of Colombia," said Mme. Choiseul, "does not have the best reputation. If I were you, I wouldn't try to recover my passport through him. Unless you plan on staying here quite a long time."

"But then what should he do?" asked Julie.

"He can have it sent directly from his country, through Rabat."

"Thank you for the advice," he said. "I'll see what I can do."

Artifo came in with a tray to pick up the cups and asked if they wanted anything more. It was already dark out, and the red fire blazed in the window panes.

XXXI

Julie was driving Mme. Choiseul's car down the narrow Monte Viejo road between the curving walls of the European mansions.

"Do you have a girlfriend?" she asked.

"No."

"Are you married?"

"No."

They arrived in silence at the "Jews' River," which runs by the foot of Monte Viejo.

"I have a friend in Colombia. We live together, but it's not going too well. How about you?"

"No, I live alone."

Now they were driving straight up Dradeb Street, a mill of activity where Muslims dashed nimbly from one curb to the other, dodging cars. The lights of the grocery shops, the foundries, and the bakeries—crowded into the ground floors of the apartment houses—shone the length of the steep street. Julie was saying it was typical of a Southern country that rich people's houses were surrounded by slums. She asked if it was that way in Cali too.

"Exactly. Can I take you to dinner?"

"I don't see why not," said Julie, smiling. "But I had the impression you had no money."

"That's true. But with a little luck I can get some cash from one of the ATMs on the Boulevard. None of them were working this morning."

"Oh, is that all it is? I thought it was more complicated. I have to confess you had me intrigued."

"Well, then, shall we go out to dinner?"

"If you like. But I have to warn you I hate Moroccan restaurants, and I don't eat fish."

"Vietnamese?"

"Why not?" But she seemed doubtful.

"I'll have to go to the pension first to drop off the owl."

Julie parked in Portugal Street, near the lower entrance to the Medina.

"Run," she said. "I'll wait here."

XXXII

He didn't like to lie but sometimes the truth about himself seemed so unacceptable that he let himself, always thinking he'd change things later so the fiction would match the reality. He *could* have been single, though in the eyes of the law he was married—since he had lived several years with his girlfriend—just as he could have been something other than an ordinary tourist with a mislaid passport. He looked in the mirror. As women were always saying, men were dogs. Smiling uncomfortably, he turned and shut the light off.

The ATM again refused to cooperate.

"It doesn't matter," said Julie. "I'll treat."

During dinner at "The Pagoda," they talked more about Moroccan politics, while several decorative carp swam up and down in the small aquarium beside them.

They came out of the restaurant onto the dark street carpeted with plastic garbage.

"Where shall we go?" Julie asked.

"You decide," he said.

"I don't suppose you'd have a little weed at your pension?"

XXXIII

Attup let them in with professional discretion.

"Excuse the mess," he said, before opening the door of his room.

The sheets were twisted up and some books lay scattered on the floor around the bed—travel guides and novels. A Moroccan ashtray full of loose tobacco and cigarette butts. Some soiled newspapers and magazines spread out at the foot of the radiator, where the owl sat. The air smelled damp.

"And this?"

A naked bulb, his reading lamp, was stuck to the wall with a piece of insulating tape.

"My own design. You can sit on the bed."

"Yes, there's nowhere else."

Now the two of them were on the bed, face to face, she with her head propped on one hand. He was emptying a cigarette. He reached out his arm to dump the tobacco in the ashtray, and took his *nabula* of kif from under the mattress. He untied it and began to fill the cigarette.

"And that?" she said, pointing to the pouch—"is that your own design too?"

"No, no. It's traditional."

He stood up to dump the ashtray in a wastebasket and came back to sit on the bed. He wet the cigarette with saliva and lit it.

XXXIV

While the kif cigarette burned down, moving back and forth between their mouths, tracing arabesques of blue smoke in the trapped air, he imagined that he was spreading cream on Julie's thigh, massaging it in with both hands.

"Oh, God," she was saying.

He was kissing her buttocks, passing his tongue over the dangerous places. He slid up her spine to her neck, biting a thick lock of her hair.

"Oh, I'm soaked."

The nipples of her smooth white breasts were curiously inverted; they grew inward; on squeezing them between his lips they emerged for a moment then sank back in the milky flesh like the retracting horns of a snail.

"It was healthy when I bought it, I'm sure of it."

"Forget it—what can you do?" she said, looking at the owl. "But it's not good here—in this room, with this humidity. It doesn't look healthy."

"Yes. It would be better in the mountains."

"Why don't you give it to me?"

"If you like."

"I'm not sure." She passed him the cigarette, and he put it out in the ashtray. "Maybe you can come with it."

"You think?"

"I'm sure." She looked at her watch. "But now I'd better go. Christine might worry. See you tomorrow?"

"I hope so."

"I'll come to look for you."

"I'll be waiting."

A quick kiss on the mouth, no saliva.

"*Au revoir, beauté,*" Julie said to the owl.

"See you tomorrow," he said.

Once alone in the room, he tore off a sheet of paper from the block he kept in his suitcase and began to write a letter home asking for money. Later in the night he had a typical dream of guilt: Swimming in a river, he saw people walking on the water, though he had to struggle hard just to stay afloat.

XXXV

Not Julie but Mme. Choiseul came to look for him the next morning. Attup led her up to his room.

"Julie's gone with Fátima to the public bath for a massage," Mme. Choiseul explained. "She asked me to pick you up. Would you like to spend a few days with us?"

They walked down toward the Avenida de España, where she had parked the car. He put his suitcase in the seat behind her and placed the owl's cage on top of it.

"In Morocco, people don't like to get to the bottom of things. No one wants to talk about something that seems wrong to us," said the voice of Nadia Yassin, the daughter of the fundamentalist leader imprisoned in Slá, who was being interviewed by Radio Medi-1.

"Let's be clear," said the interviewer. "What you people want is revolution."

"No," said the young woman. "But we do want radical change. And we don't just want to change *things*; we want to change *mankind*."

"What do you think?" asked Mme. Choiseul, turning off the radio.

"She's not stupid."

"She sounds like a French high-school student."

They drove on in silence, getting farther away from the center of Tangier, heading toward the Zoco de los Bueyes. They went down California and kept on toward Monte Viejo on Vasco da Gama.

The little Pekingese met them at the front door.

"Follow me. I'll show you your bedroom. I hope you like it." She smiled.

The bedroom was in the lowest part of the garden, a little cottage in Moorish style, flanked by Roman cypresses. Inside, it was generously carpeted; cushions of various sizes and colors were piled on the bed. In one corner, a small fireplace waited to be lit. Through an arched window one could see, in the distance, the hump of Mount M'Jimet, dotted with little cubical houses.

"What do you think?"

"It's wonderful."

Mme. Choiseul set the cage down on a small inlaid table near the window. The owl was listening attentively, now with one ear, now the other, to what was going on around it.

"This is the life," he said to himself when he was alone, lying on the bed with his hands crossed behind his head. Beyond the window mullion and the cypresses, hundreds of starlings and sparrows were crying and streaking the blue-gold of afternoon.

"It can't last," he thought.

XXXVI

Julie, with her small prow-like face, walked beside him on the white sand beach, which faded in the distance to the south of Ras Achakar. There lay the ruins of Cotta, she said, where, for centuries, the Romans had pressed olives for oil and seasoned sardines and tuna.

"This is where they cut off the heads, entrails, fins, and tails, which they used to make fish paste," Julie explained. "The floor was built of perfectly hewn flagstones—there are still some fragments." She wanted to continue the excavations that Princess Rúspoli had started in the 1950s and that the Moroccan government had forced her to abandon after Independence.

They had walked past a large heap of stones, each one numbered (by order of the deceased princess, Julie said) like pieces of a huge jigsaw puzzle, which one day would all fit together to rebuild the Roman baths. Over the sea hung a hazy castle of dust, its colors mixing and changing hue in the western sun.

"Maybe I'll come back next year," Julie said. "But I'd need a permit from His Cherifian Majesty, and I don't think I'll get it, unless Christine talks to somebody in Rabat. At any rate, next week I'm going to start a course in Maghrebi Arabic. Without the language, I don't think I can accomplish much."

"I envy you." He took her hand.

Julie gave him a solemn smile.

"Your wife—," she said then, without looking at him, "doesn't it bother you to cheat on her?"

"Yes, but I don't have any choice."

"That's hard for me to understand."

In the past, a phrase from Chamfort had worked for him:

"Laura," he said, "is the kind of woman it's impossible not to cheat on."

"What does that mean?" Julie asked, somewhat offended.

"That she's the kind of woman it's impossible to leave." He smiled.

"Oh, I see," said Julie in a low voice. Then, between her teeth: "*Imbécile.*"

She stopped, turning on her heels.

"What's wrong?"

"Nothing."

"Are you annoyed?"

"No."

They walked in silence, casting long shadows on the sand, toward the rock embankment at the end of the beach where they'd left the car.

XXXVII

Failing to find Rashid at the Tingis, he walked down to the port and took a taxi.

"To the Boulevard?"

"No, to Monte Viejo, please," he said in Maghrebi. "Do you know where it is?"

"Yes," said the driver and looked at him. "Are you Moroccan?"

"No."

"Tunisian?"

"No."

"Egyptian?"

"No."

"Where are you from?"

"Colombia."

"But they speak Arabic in Colombia?"

"No. Spanish."

"We speak Spanish here too," said the driver in Tangerine Spanish. "What's it like in your country?"

"More or less like here."

"Horrible, in other words."

"That's about it."

The radio was broadcasting a Moroccan football game. The driver asked if they bet on sports in Colombia.

"Not as much as they do here."

"It's an interesting game. You can win a lot of money."

"If you're lucky, I guess."

"I think you are a lucky man."

"I don't know," he said. "Luck comes and goes."

"You're right there, my friend."

The Mercedes turned rather dangerously down the slope toward the California district.

"You are learning Arabic."

"I'd like to."

"Do you like Morocco?"

"Very much."

"There you are. Do you know what Islam is?"

"Of course."

"No, I'm asking if you know what it really is. Are you a Muslim?"

"No, no. I'm a Christian."

"How are you going to know what Islam is if you're not a Muslim?"

"You have a point."

"Well. If you want to, you can convert to Islam. You only need to say . . ."

"Yes, I know. It's been explained to me."

"Well, *khay*—then you will understand. You're not a Jew, are you?"

"No."

"Well, then, there is no problem. If you want to, you can become a Muslim."

They continued along Vasco da Gama toward the Sidi Mesmudi road and passed in front of the country estate of one of the princesses of Kuwait.

"Here only the very rich live," said the driver with contempt. He felt a strange shame on behalf of the rich.

"Here it is," he said when they arrived at Mme. Choiseul's home.

"Here?" The driver stopped the Mercedes in front of the door. "That's a hundred dirhams," he said.

"How's that?"

"*Mía dirham.* One hundred dirhams."

"That's way too much."

"Too much? Well, give me eighty."

"Twenty is what I'm used to paying."

The driver, without looking at him, shook his head. "All right, fifty."

"Thirty," he replied, counting his coins, "thirty is all I'm going to give you."

He stretched out his hand with the money, but the driver would not take it. He stepped out of the taxi, leaving the money on the seat. He was closing the door when the driver screamed furiously:

"*Intina yehudi!*"

On the Tangier side, thousands of swallows were taking flight in a block against the huge screen of the sky, each one a point in a net that was changing its form, weaving and unweaving at the whim of some natural intelligence.

XXXVIII

The owl opened its eyes onto the hungry, liquid light of the dusk. It turned one ear toward the window, better to hear the sounds that filled the air of the sunset and mixed with the steady murmur of the breeze rising from the sea. A man was shouting, as he did every afternoon at this time. The birds continued scratching the sky or crying from the branches. Several mosquitoes buzzed near the window and some moths began to flutter close, drawn by the sun's last rays in the window panes. A lizard's skin scraped as it crawled through a crevice under the window. The dry leaves, the dust, a dead beetle—all were swept up by the wind. A grasshopper flew over the lawn. The old Moroccan who tended the fire carried out the meaningless movements he always made at this hour—you could hear the sound of his feet and knees shifting on the straw mat.

The man who fed it meat was talking with someone—the sound of their voices came through very faintly, drowned in the snore of an automobile engine. The stranger raised his voice, and the sound of the car moved off. The little dog was barking. Someone drew near on the stone path that descended from the upper garden.

The owl recognized the sound of the footsteps of the person approaching: it was the boy who had wakened it from its light sleep earlier in the afternoon by tapping his finger on the window pane. "Yuk, yuk," was the sound the boy had made, which startled it. It had once heard another boy make the same sound.

That was when the owl lived in the ruins of the old Italian

hospital. The cornice where it had made its nest looked over an unkempt garden, with rows of flowers grown into thickets, and creepers hanging from the branches. It had felt safe there, since no one, neither nuns nor monks, had walked in that garden for many years. From the other side of the garden, next to the railing that separated it from the street, there used to be a large kennel where a police dog was kept and where one day a Moroccan boy moved in. He was from the country and had the rustic ways of country people. He must have seen the owl return to its nest one morning, because later he climbed up to the cornice with a ladder to surprise it while it was sleeping. He threw a gunny sack over it and tied its feet with a rope. The owl, quivering at the memory, let out a screech. It was awake now, but it was helpless.

XXXIX

"Yoohoo, up here!" came the voice of Mme. Choiseul from a balcony. "How did it go?"

"*Comme ci, comme ça,*" he said, looking upward. "Hasn't Julie come back?"

"Yes, she came back. But she's gone shopping, something last-minute. We invited some friends to dinner. A Belgian girl married to a Moroccan. If you'd like to join us, you're most welcome."

"Yes, delighted. Thanks."

"They'll be coming at seven."

"Can I help you with something?"

"No, no. Everything's set."

"You're sure?"

"Well, if you insist—how would you like to cut some flowers from the garden?"

XL

The night smelled of the jasmine he had cut. He pushed open the door of the guest house and, seeing the window open and the cage empty, felt a sensation of loss which—he told himself—had nothing to do with a mere owl. He looked under the bed, and a current of cold air grazed his head. He went to shut the window, which he was sure he had not left open. He noted the firewood in the basket and thought of Artifo: maybe he could explain it. He looked through the window at the darkness outside, accented by the distant glow of lights on the hilltops on the far side of the Bay of Tangier, which for a moment he had confused with stars.

He left the house and walked around it, looking for some sign of the bird. If it had leapt out the window, it might still be nearby. He walked toward the main house, and, halfway up, stopped to listen: Mme. Choiseul and Julie were discussing something in one of the upstairs rooms, but he couldn't make out what they were saying. He walked around the house and ran into Artifo near the room where the wood was stored.

"Excuse me, Artifo. Have you been in my room?"

"Not yet, sir."

"Who brought the wood, do you know?"

"I don't know. Maybe it was Fátima. Have you run out? I'll bring some more."

"No, thank you. It's not that. Someone opened the window—it wasn't you?"

"No, sir."

"Who might have opened it?"

Artifo shrugged his shoulders, as if to ask why anyone would be worried about an open window.

"The owl has escaped," he said. "Have you seen it?"

"No. Wasn't it in its cage?"

"I left it out of its cage."

"Ah. Why did you leave it out?"

"Because . . . Forget it." He turned around, holding his anger.

XLI

"Don't forget we're in Morocco," said Mrs. Sebti, setting the salad platter within reach of her hostess. "Didn't you know the law here forbids and punishes relations between men and women if they're not married?"

"Only between men and women, eh?" said Mme. Choiseul, looking at Adil es-Sebti, the Moroccan husband.

Meanwhile Adil was telling Julie:

"Of course, but just like the sardine paste, the olive oil came from *here*. In Cádiz it was poured into amphorae made there and was shipped that way to Rome. The *maquila* was invented a long time ago, my dear friend . . ."

From the ocean the sound of a motorboat rose up. They all heard it.

"Smugglers," said Adil.

They sat awhile listening—the sound moved away from the coast—then returned to their conversations.

"You're Muslim, aren't you?" said Julie to Mrs. Sebti.

"It's automatic, if you marry a Moroccan."

"But it's a bit absurd," said Mme. Choiseul. "They don't believe in anyone converting, unless for some reason it's convenient for them. As in this case: in order to appropriate the enemy's wife." She smiled. "Clan mentality. Pardon me, Adil, but that's how I see it."

"What are the Colombian women like?" asked Mrs. Sebti, to include him in the conversation.

He was thinking of the owl.

"Excuse me?"

"Are the Colombian women terribly Catholic," she smiled ambiguously, "or are they emancipated?"

"There are all kinds," he answered.

"Like here."

"Maybe. Maybe here they're more traditional."

"Are they like the Spanish?"

"And what is that supposed to mean?" Mme. Choiseul interrupted.

"So open," smiled Adil.

"I couldn't tell you," he said. "I don't know Spanish women very well." He turned to Julie and said, "The owl is gone. The window was open, but I was sure I shut it."

Mme. Choiseul was saying to Adil:

"I agree, perhaps they aren't any happier. Still, it seems to me that it's worth trying." Then she turned toward him to say, "The owl? Really?" She thought a moment. "You're not missing anything else? Money, jewelry?"

"No. Nothing."

"Artifo's grandson . . ." Mme. Choiseul decided not to continue; the others were still talking about the emancipation of the Moroccan people. Then: "I saw him prowling around your room. Let's ask Artifo about it later."

"No, no," Adil was saying. "They should put all undocumented blacks in jail. They're a real problem."

Julie was furious.

"You may know about sardines and olive oil," she said, "but

your opinions on other matters won't get you very far in Europe or anywhere else in the civilized world."

"I don't plan to change countries," said Adil, smiling a bit bitterly, "nor religions, so what you're saying is not a problem for me."

Mrs. Sebti looked at her husband with disapproval.

"I think I want to go get some sleep. Shall we go?" she said to him.

Mme. Choiseul walked them to the door, while Julie, who seemed nervous, cleared off some glasses and took them into the kitchen. She returned with several bottles of beer on a tray.

"Have one?" she asked, and he stretched out his hand to take a bottle. "Christine's asking Artifo about Hamsa, his grandson. It seems he's the one who took the owl."

Mme. Choiseul returned, her face showing satisfaction. She sat down near the fire and poured herself half a glass of beer.

"I think the mystery is solved," she said.

XLII

They went on foot, following Artifo on the road between the high walls of the Saudi palaces, spiked with sharpened metal points and broken bottle shards, while the wind hummed along the electrical wires. The last wall ended abruptly in an avalanche of garbage that fell down the hillside toward the sea among a thin grove of cedars. They could hear the sea, aniline blue, crashing on the shore. Two crows and, farther down, two poor women wearing black kerchiefs and turquoise and tangerine-colored djellabas rummaged purposefully through the dump.

They passed a ravine and a large house with a broken well wheel, where the view opened gloriously onto the steep green slopes leading to the nipple of rock that was Cape Spartel.

They were walking now along an old cobblestone road across a clover pasture spattered with goat and sheep dung. Coming to a stone hut, painted blue and surrounded with brambles on which clothes were hung to dry, Artifo stopped and shouted someone's name. There was no answer.

They climbed a path carved in the rock, toward the ruins of the Perdicaris mansion, then turned onto a downward trail. On a small flat horseshoe of rock they found the shepherd's stone hut, its canvas roof blackened with tar and iron sulfate.

Neither Hamsa nor the sheep were there.

"He won't be long," said Artifo.

They sat down on the grass looking at the sea, which crashed against the piled rocks fifty meters below the cliff from which they had fallen.

Before long they heard the sound of hooves on stones. From between two crags came the herd of sheep. The first of them stopped a moment to look with curious, benevolent eyes at the strangers; then, pushed on by those who came behind, they trotted toward the stone and thorn corral.

"*Derrrrr!*" shouted Hamsa, who appeared at the rear.

When all the sheep were inside, he shut the door of the corral and counted them. Without hurrying, he went to greet his grandfather.

Artifo spoke to him in Maghrebi.

"Can you ask him if he took the owl?" he interrupted. Artifo looked annoyed and shook his head.

"Wait, wait."

Soon Artifo began to interrogate the boy, who seemed indifferent. He heard Mme. Choiseul's name pronounced, and finally Hamsa nodded his head. He looked out for a few seconds at the layer of fog that covered the Spanish coast, and then, in a tone quite different from that he had been using, began to explain. When he had finished talking, Artifo returned to the foreigners and said gravely:

"Yes, he has the owl."

"All right," he replied, without anger, "where is it?"

Another exchange in Maghrebi. Then Hamsa went to open the little door of the hut, lifting the cloth with his staff so that the visitors did not have to bend down too far to pass inside.

When his eyes had grown accustomed to the darkness, he saw the owl on its stake, its head folded on its chest. He turned toward Artifo, who seemed relieved.

"Did he tell you why he took it?" he asked.

The owl raised its head and looked around.

Hamsa made more explanations to his grandfather. The latter interpreted, addressing Julie instead of looking at him.

"He didn't know it belonged to anyone," he said. "He saw it in the window and since it was hurt, he thought it had stopped there for shelter, and he caught it."

"And the cage?" he said. "Didn't he see the cage?"

"He says he didn't."

"What did he plan to do with it?"

"Heal it and then let it go."

"Can't he sell it?"

Now Artifo looked at him.

"Owls aren't worth anything."

He's lying, he thought. But what would he want with an owl?

"Really?"

"They're not worth much," Artifo corrected himself. "The children catch them sometimes to sell to an old woman or a Jew who'll use them for witchcraft."

He looked at Julie.

"What do you think?"

The shepherd put on an innocent face. He was obviously a simpleton, but it looked as if he meant well.

"If he thinks he can cure it," Julie said, "why not leave it here so he can try?"

He didn't think Hamsa was capable of curing it. Still, "Yes," he said. "Why not?"

He turned to Artifo.

"I'll leave it here."

In parting, Julie gave her hand to Hamsa and he followed her example and then crouched in front of the owl and touched its head softly to say goodbye. The owl shook its head.

He came out of the hut behind Julie. The day was at its brightest, the sky was streaked with cirrus clouds from horizon to horizon. They began to walk, breathing the blue, lustrous air. Julie took his arm with affectionate authority.

"I think you did the right thing."

"I suppose," he said doubtfully.

Artifo came out of the hut hurriedly and caught up with them.

"*Monsieur*," he said, "my grandson asks if you can spare a little money to buy meat for the bird."

He snorted, but with a smile of indulgence. He took out a twenty-dirham bill from his pants pocket and gave it to Artifo, who returned hastily to the hut.

Julie took his arm again and they walked uphill without waiting for the old Moroccan.

"Did I already tell you," Julie was saying, "that the nine thousand lions the Romans sacrificed at the dedication of the Colosseum were all Moroccan? They sent them over from Volúbilis. They managed to wipe them all out in less than two centuries."

When they reached the high point of the road, he stopped and looked west, where the sea opened. With some sadness, he felt he might be seeing the place for the last time.

XLIII

Thinking of Julie, he walked quickly down toward the Zoco Chico, along Plateros Street, where vendors were selling hard taffy and Moorish crepes. Thanks to Julie, he knew this street had once been a Roman causeway.

At the Café Tingis, Rashid was sitting with a group of friends, as usual, filling out football cards.

"Betis, Atlético de Bilbao . . . Mallorca, Salamanca . . . Real Madrid, Barcelona . . . ," they recited.

Rashid saw him, said, "Just a moment," and turned back to the cards.

He went to eye the window display in a shop across the plaza, where in ancient times a Roman forum had stood. Would a Moroccan amber necklace make Laura happy? Maybe, he thought; but he didn't have enough money.

"Hey, *amigo!*" shouted Rashid, who had got up from his gambling and crossed the small plaza to meet him.

"What's new? You haven't forgotten Rashid, eh? You want your watch?" He laughed. "Have you got my money?" He squeezed his hand.

"No. You can keep the watch." He looked at Rashid's wrist but didn't see any watch. "I came to say goodbye. My passport is on the way."

"Let's have a coffee. This time I'll treat."

They left the Zoco Chico and headed down toward the Café Stah.

"It's a pity you're going. I was thinking of asking you a big favor," said Rashid when they were seated in the sun on the café terrace. The smooth golden light off the bay that bathed their eyes, the horn of a ship leaving the port, the smell of black tobacco smoke and coffee—all this gave a nostalgic flavor to the farewell conversation. "I'm sure I'll win this bet. We filled it out among a few friends. I was thinking: the only person I'd trust to go to Spain to cash it is you."

"It would be an honor," he said. "If I weren't leaving, I'd gladly do you the favor."

"*Insha Al-láh.*"

A few minutes later they got up and walked toward the port.

"And what about the owl?" Rashid asked.

They said goodbye in front of the taxi station, agreeing that, if he didn't leave this week, he'd come back to see if Rashid and his friends had won their wager.

"If we win," said Rashid, "you'll go over to Algeciras to collect the money. It will be wonderful. We'll give you a five percent commission, that's a promise."

"All right then," he said.

"*Hasta luego,*" said Rashid, and embraced him with a kiss on each cheek. "And *Trek salama!* if you go."

THE NECKLACE

XLIV

My dear love,

I'm writing you on a computer to save space. What a bother this passport stuff is, and it's stretching out the time till we can be together! I went to the embassy and spoke with the first secretary. Monday they'll tell me something, but they've warned me the paperwork can take a long time. It literally makes my heart sink just to think of it.

I told your uncle. He's not happy, you know him—always so distrustful. He says he's going to dock your pay for every day you miss. If you weren't one of his favorite nephews, he'd have fired you already—that's what he says.

I called last night at Solano's house, but Victor hadn't come back yet. Apparently the plane was delayed in Madrid.

Be good.

XLV

My love,

Thanks a million for the slippers and the caftan, which Victor brought over on Saturday, soon after he got back. They fit me perfectly.

On Monday we went with the Solanos on an impromptu visit—in Victor's father's small plane—to the Chocó park, since it was Victor's birthday, as you know. The first hour we were there, it was as though all the animals decided to come out to greet Victor. We saw everything: two little foxes, tobacco- and orange-colored, some spider monkeys, two toucans, a coatimundi, a lizard that had the bad luck to be eaten before our eyes by a snake. And thousands, literally thousands of sulphur-colored butterflies—drifting through the jungle, moving south. They kept on going for hours—in fact, the whole time we were there. Victor said this could be a harbinger of bad weather.

I phoned the first secretary this morning, but he was in a meeting. He hasn't returned my call.

XLVI

My darling,

Your uncle phoned today, he was worried about your news. Victor's going to fill in for you—just until you're back, he assures me. I told him I talked to the embassy people, and he says he's going to put some pressure on the secretary, but I think it could be a mistake. The secretary, don Sebastián Vichiria, is a nasty old creep, as your friend Blanca would say, and has some incredible prejudices. He seems to disapprove of your deciding to lose your passport in a place like Tangier. He says everyone knows it's one of the sin capitals of the world. He refuses to deal with the honorary consul, whom you've visited, saying he's a North American with the worst kind of reputation, and wants us to take care of everything through the embassy, which is in Rabat. He had the nerve to ask me if it wasn't possible that you had sold (or given) your passport to a Moroccan; according to him, there are lots of cases like that. Is it true that many Moroccans die every day trying to cross the strait?

Well, my sweet. Take care of yourself, don't get too bored, and think of me.

XLVII

Hello precious!

Where are you? I called the Hotel Atlas—I can dial direct, contrary to what you told me—and they said you'd moved out.

Your uncle spoke with Vichiria, but things have gotten complicated.

Now he has suggested, in all seriousness, that you might be involved in running drugs. I don't know what I'm going to do. You feel so far away. Your last fax seemed to me very cold. I hope our next meeting will bring back some wild passion with it.

Of course, I deposited more money in your account as you asked me to. But remember I'm not swimming in cash, and it's worse now with the telephone rate gone up and my sending you all these faxes.

XLVIII

My beloved,

The bit about moving out of the Atlas because of an owl is original. But it's not funny that you write only to ask for money. What are you doing all day? I repeat: you don't need to be jealous of Victor or anyone else.

You can't imagine the damage the hurricane has caused. People say it was almost as bad as Mitch. Three days ago they declared a national emergency. Nobody, at least here in Cali, has gone to work. The Solanos and I decided to travel to the Chocó this weekend (strange as it seems, the weather there is superb, according to Victor's friends, who have a boarding house right in the park, on the edge of the Atrato) instead of staying here to watch it rain in Cali. Hundreds of people died on the coast, thousands lost their houses, and the streets are really bad.

I feel so worried, not knowing what to do and wondering when I'm going to see you.

XLIX

Hello!

Last night I got back late from the trip and found only a few lines from your last fax. The paper had run out and I'd forgotten to change the roll—I've been so adrift. Can you send it again?

A Mr. Lavarría called you. It seems he has lost his house and needs help. Your uncle is beside himself, extremely upset with you. His warehouses are flooded more than a meter deep in mud, which now appears to be hardening. To clean it up will take months of work and a great deal of money. He says that, if you had wanted to, you could have gotten a safe-conduct to return immediately, and that you requested the passport in order to prolong your vacation.

I've got to go.

L

Hi my love,

Doctor Vichiria just phoned to ask me for money to send your passport by special courier to Tangier, to the house of one Mme. Choiseul. It's a hundred dollars, which I don't know where I'm going to find.

I have to tell you there have been changes here, some of them drastic.

The one that will affect you most, I think, is that your uncle has hired Victor to fill the position that you've left vacant for almost a month. I phoned him to tell him it doesn't seem fair, but he hasn't called back. I guess he doesn't want to talk to me.

Begonia and Victor are separating—rather, they have already split up: she left him.

And (it literally breaks my heart to write it) I am leaving this apartment tonight, I think for good.

Part Three

FLIGHT

LI

It was clear that whoever was following him had slipped through Spanish customs. The smugglers did it all the time; everyone knew it. It had been a mistake to accept Rashid's proposition. Even if he had been offered ten percent of the money, it would have been a mistake.

He was almost sure it was one of the Moroccans he had seen filling out the betting cards with Rashid. Now, while the Spanish recruits were getting noisily drunk on beer and homesickness, the Moroccan was playing pinball at the other end of the Bodegas Melilla.

He picked up his beer from the bar and turned to look at a Moroccan girl. She was truly beautiful. She had fair hair and gray eyes. She was talking to a Spaniard with thick skin and deep wrinkles and the hoarse, almost metallic voice of an inveterate smoker. The girl was either a smuggler or a prostitute—or both, he thought.

He turned toward the large mirror behind the bar. Rashid had trusted him; now he distrusted Rashid. But that wouldn't justify his disappearing after collecting the money instead of returning to Tangier. If they were following him, it was to prevent that. He slipped two fingers in the hidden pocket of his pants and felt the edge of the ticket. Fifty million pesetas was too much money.

Where did he catch up with me? he wondered. Foreseeing just such a ploy, he had changed his plans at the last minute. Instead of catching the ferry from Tangier to Algeciras, as he had told Rashid he would do, he took a bus to Melilla. He had left the pension at dawn, three hours earlier than planned, and he was sure no one had followed him to the station. But Attup could have alerted them.

After ordering another beer, and touching his chest pocket where he kept his new passport, he looked again at the beautiful Moroccan girl. She became aware of him and gave him a furtive smile. The Spaniard was explaining something to her, eyes fixed on the floor covered with sawdust and cigarette butts.

It would be absurd to die in Melilla, he thought.

He didn't want to get drunk, and it was too early to sleep. He left the Bodegas Melilla and turned the corner at Juan Carlos I, instead of returning toward Primo de Rivera and his hotel.

He walked as far as the Plaza de España, looking back from time to time, but he didn't see the Moroccan. The streets began to get livelier; the siesta hour was past. As in Tangier, human activity here was cheered by the cries and twitters of birds.

The Plaza de España had a Catalán flavor, but the tiles and stucco facades couldn't offset the ugliness of the garish advertisements for travel agencies and other businesses. Although he had already bought a ticket for the ferry to Almería, at that moment he decided to change it for one to Málaga. He went into an agency on Pablo Valesca Street and, confirming that the difference in price between the ferry and the plane was negligible, decided to fly to Málaga. It would be more difficult to follow him, he thought—if in fact someone was following him.

But it was absurd to keep thinking this, he told himself, as he came out onto the street and looked in all directions, trying to spot the Moroccan among the Spanish crowd. He walked up the esplanade of General Macías toward Medina Sidonia, drawn by an unaccountable nostalgia, that sense of loss that he had felt only in Tangier.

He turned up a winding street toward the chapel of Santiago el Matamoros, until he came to a small fort that reminded him of the fort of Xáuen but that turned out to be the municipal museum. It was closed, so he walked the length of the rampart and found a little Moroccan market. He remembered the day he'd gone with Julie to Xáuen. A little after that, the Frenchwomen had gone back to Paris, practically leaving him in the street. He could understand that Mme. Choiseul wouldn't invite him to stay in her house. Still, he had entertained the fantasy. Afterward, he spent several weeks waiting for news from Julie, and one day he finally got some: she had a new boyfriend in Paris. Would he still be in Tangier in the spring when she planned to come back? Probably not, he answered; he didn't hear from her again.

To avoid the stairs he'd taken on the way up, he walked down to the Plaza de la Avanzadilla by a dark lane that came to a fork; the branch he chose, the wider, like so many lanes in the Tangier Medina, went on narrowing little by little, until it turned into a kind of family courtyard. A black cat was chewing noisily on a piece of fish. Shouts came from a window, then a child's laughter.

He turned to go back up the lane, when the Moroccan, who must have been following him at a distance all this time, blocked the way.

"Excuse me," he said in panic. His gut clenched.

The other didn't move.

"Do we know each other?" His voice sounded broken. He swallowed acid saliva.

"You bet I know you, *hombre*." An unexpected accent.

"Really?" He inhaled. "Sorry, I don't remember. What was your name?"

"Ángel Tejedor," said the other very clearly.

"How's that?" Something strange happened inside him. The burning he felt in all his pores was adrenalin from the shock. His legs began to tremble, slightly but uncontrollably. This, Ángel Tejedor, was his own name. "Is this a joke?" he managed to say.

"No joke."

He backed up two paces. He felt a sharp cramp in his stomach.

"What do you want?"

"Nothing."

"Rashid sent you?"

The other shook his head. He took a long knife from under his jacket.

"Let's have it," he said. "The passport and the ticket."

He took the ticket out first; then, reluctantly, his passport.

"Put the ticket inside the passport and throw it on the ground here beside me. Right here beside me."

Then he told him to take off his shoes. Curiously, this calmed him. The Moroccan took his shoes and threw them high in the air. He could hear them fall on a rooftop.

"Get down on your stomach."

He started to obey, bending forward, but all at once he understood that the man was going to kill him, that he had to kill him if he was going to become him. He flung himself forward against him, and they fell to the ground in each other's arms. An unknown, unpleasant odor. But there was something liberating, almost pleasurable in the elemental struggle: his fear dissolved. The black cat shot up the alley. His hands turned into claws, and his enemy's long hair into an advantage as he seized it hard and yanked it, knocking the man's skull against the street—twice, with a *crack*. He was a crossroads of colors and pulsations, and perhaps the thread of blood he saw oozing between the uneven cobblestones toward the bottom of the alley was not his own.

His hand came up against a bland, rectangular object. The passport. Without quite believing it, he jumped up and went running up the alley. Only once did he look back, before turning the first corner. The man seemed to move.

LII

In reality it was Ismail who cured the owl, which he called Sarsara. First he covered its wing with a poultice of sheep dung. Later, removing the poultice, he gently grasped the broken part of the wing and tied two ribbons around it, one red and one blue, from which he hung a porcupine jawbone. And while Hamsa was away taking care of the sheep, he sang it healing songs, which he had learned from his mother, or which he invented:

> *"The day that you had twins,*
> *they broke your wing."*
> *"But I never had twins!"*
> *"And they never broke your wing."*

Now the owl could fly. Ismail took it out of the hut in the evening, tied by a fishing line around one of its feet. Little by little, he gave it more line, and the owl circled around him, close to the ground, in its silent great-winged flight.

"If it gets away," Hamsa told him, "you're going to pay for it. I'll cut out *your* eyes!"

Once, the owl perched in the branches of an old olive tree, and Ismail let it stay there. Suddenly, the owl flew a few meters away, veered and dived onto the ground, which was covered with dead leaves. Then it returned to its olive bough, with a little mouse in its claws, which, Ismail could see from a distance, it swallowed in one gulp.

LIII

Seven months had passed since the theft of the owl. It was the time of *nissan*, in May, the propitious time when everyone is supposed to be happy, but this year no rain had fallen. There were no storks on the roofs, and the snakes had not come out of their holes. The fields were dry, the animals sickly.

Ismail was growing up and beginning to rebel against Hamsa. One afternoon, after tying the owl to its stake inside the hut, Hamsa had thrown himself upon him and Ismail had slipped out from under his *casheb* and gone running out of the hut. Hamsa had not followed him. He had stayed on the ground smiling, hearing the boy scream and hurl insults at him from high in the rocks.

The owl didn't bother Hamsa. He was used to its insistent gaze and even to its song which, people said, brought death. He was just waiting for word from his uncle to carry out the sacrifice, since he was afraid the amulet might lose its power with time. A year might pass before he was back—his uncle had said when he left—and now the year had gone by.

On the afternoon that the Christian woman visited him, Hamsa was sitting alone eating a plate of ground almonds with honey and cinnamon.

"*Salaam aleikum,*" she called from outside.

Hamsa came out of the hut.

"*Aleikum salaam,*" he said.

"Do you remember me?" the woman asked in Maghrebi.

Hamsa said yes with surprise, and since she didn't say anything more, added:

"You came to see me with my grandfather and another Nazarene."

The Christian woman smiled. The sun was falling on the edge of Monte Viejo, casting its rays between the black cedar trunks.

"You live in a beautiful place," she said.

An oil tanker disappeared in the thick fog of the strait. Hamsa said:

"I was going to have tea. Do you want to come in?"

"Thank you," she answered, hesitating. "The bird—do you still have it?"

"The yuca? It's inside," he said. He closed his eyes and turned his head toward the little half-open door.

"Have you cured it?"

Hamsa nodded his head.

"Really?"

"It can fly now."

"Can I see it?"

"Come in."

He turned, pushed the door open, and with one hand lifted the black cloth of the doorway.

LIV

"Tu-uit tu-hu," said the owl. It turned its head and looked at the woman, who drew near slowly so as not to startle it.

"How are you?"

The owl raised its wings as if to demonstrate that it was cured. It opened its beak.

"Bravo," said the woman to Hamsa with an admiring look.

Hamsa smiled.

"*Báraca,*" he said. "Do you want to drink tea?"

"Thanks."

Hamsa pointed to the skins where the Christian woman could sit. He lit a gas burner.

"Your grandfather asked me to bring you some news," she said.

Hamsa looked at her suspiciously. No Moroccan wants to be the bearer of bad tidings, so the fact that Artifo was sending news by means of this woman disturbed him.

"It's about your uncle Jalid."

Hamsa's eyes widened.

"Is he coming?" he asked.

"He would come," the Christian woman said. "He would come—if he weren't under arrest in Algeciras."

"In jail?"

"That's what your grandfather said."

"Why?"

"I don't know."

"Do you know when he'll get out?"

"He didn't tell me. But I don't think it will be soon."

Hamsa put fresh mint in a brass teapot, added sugar, took two glasses and put them on the small round table.

"*Hamdul-láh*," he said at last; there was nothing he could do. "Are you Spanish?" he asked.

"No. I'm French."

Hamsa turned his face toward Spain.

"*Hijos de puta!*" he said between his teeth.

He lifted the kettle of boiling water and poured it over the tea. The smell of mint rose up with the steam.

"When will you let the owl go?"

"I don't know."

"Have you grown fond of it?"

Hamsa laughed.

"No, not at all."

"So, why don't you let it go?"

"I might need it," he said.

"What for?"

"I can't tell you."

"A secret?" she said in French; she didn't know the Maghrebi word.

Hamsa mentally calculated the likely price of an owl, and he wondered how much he would have to pay for a woman like her. Would she go to bed with him in exchange for the yuca? But it was not an easy proposition to make. If she desired him, there would be no problem. If he could manage to put a little saliva on her glass, maybe he could get what he wanted.

"Do you live here alone?"

"Yes."

"It's very nice here," she said, and looked around her. She took off her pullover.

Hamsa tried the tea, smacking his lips, then put it back on the table.

"I need a few things," he said. "Someday I'll have a real house. That will be better."

"Of course."

Hamsa crouched in front of the table and, hiding the glasses for an instant with his body, let a drop of spit fall into the glass that would be hers. Then he lifted the steaming teapot and served the tea, which made a little foam as it poured into the glasses.

"Here," he said, handing her the glass.

"Don't you want to sell me the owl?"

Hamsa moved his head ambiguously, not saying yes or no.

"What do you say?" insisted the woman.

"How much would you pay?"

"I don't know, you'd better tell me how much you want."

"I would like to kiss you," he said.

Hamsa felt himself blush, and the woman's nostrils flared.

"Kiss me?" she exclaimed, confused, pointing to herself with her forefinger. "You're crazy."

"Excuse me, excuse me. That's what I want, that's all," Hamsa said, noticing her small but erect breasts covered only by her cotton undershirt.

"Forget it," said the woman, shaking her head slightly.

Hamsa looked down at his feet. He was wearing his Nikes, now very battered.

"Two hundred dirhams," she persisted.

Hamsa, without taking his eyes from the ground, shook his head no.

"Are you sure? Who else will buy it?"

"I don't want money," he assured her, staring at her. "I don't care about money." He poured more tea.

The Christian woman drank silently, observing him with curiosity.

"Three hundred?"

If she weren't interested, if she were angry, she'd have left by now, Hamsa thought. The spell of the saliva was working. *She's giving me another chance*, he reasoned.

"For each feather in the owl," he said, encouraged, "I want a kiss."

The Christian woman laughed.

"It is a tempting offer, I'm sure," she said, smiling nervously. "That's a lot of kisses."

Hamsa crouched a little, looking anxiously at the foreigner's feet. She had taken off her slippers before sitting on the sheepskin rug. Her feet were delicate and very white. Hamsa leaned over further, as if to kiss them; she didn't move them.

"No, no, Hamsa," she protested, when his lips touched the cold skin of her foot. She drew them back then, hugging her knees. "That's enough, now."

Her body was trembling slightly, Hamsa realized. He served a bit more tea, then stretched out one hand to reach his *motui*, which hung on a hook over his head. He assembled his kif pipe in silence, filled it, and smoked.

"Do you smoke?" He offered it to the Christian woman.

"Thanks, yes." She took the pipe, smoked, and began to cough. "It has tobacco," she protested.

"It has to have it," said Hamsa, surprised, and smoked again.

"Let's see, I'll try it again," said the Christian. Hamsa gave her the pipe. This time she drew on it slowly and didn't choke. "It's good kif," she acknowledged. She took a sip of tea.

"I wonder," she said a few minutes later, lying back on the skins, "how many feathers an owl would have."

That was a good sign, Hamsa said to himself. The Christian woman desired him. He stretched out his hand to stroke her foot, and she let him. Hamsa said,

"How many kisses do you think I can give you?"

"Quite a few, I imagine," she said.

LV

"Two hundred?"

"I don't know. I stopped counting."

Hamsa made her lie down on the skins.

"Wait," she said firmly. "First, set the owl free."

"*Uaja, uaja.*" He got up and went over to crouch down in front of the bird, whose head turned to look at the woman, stretched out on the sheepskins, while Hamsa's nervous hands untied the knot that held it.

When it was free, it flew toward a corner of the hut and perched on a wooden sawhorse, out of the shepherd's reach. It hooted.

The Christian woman said:

"Open the door."

Hamsa said no. "*You* will open it. Afterward."

The owl flew from the sawhorse to the door, always out of the shepherd's reach, then spun rapidly back to its stake. The Christian woman looked at Hamsa, who was kneeling next to her. Hamsa took off his gandura and unbuttoned his baggy breeches.

"Oh, Hamsa," she said and sat up on the sheepskin. She looked with surprise at the shepherd's circumcised member, which was enormous.

Hamsa went on undressing.

"What's the matter?" he said.

She had drawn back and looked alarmed.

There was a stain the size of a pea, of a ruddy grayish color, on one of his swarthy little sacks that seemed to breathe with its own life. In the center, where a hair was growing, was something that looked like pus.

Hamsa looked at it himself.

"That's nothing," he asserted, gruffly. "Come on, take off your clothes."

"Hamsa, I'm sorry, really. You'll hurt me with that." In one jump, she had stood up.

"Come here," said Hamsa, trying to grab her by the arm.

"Hamsa, I'm sorry, it's not going to happen. Keep the owl. Excuse me, I'm going."

"No!" Hamsa tried to grab her, but she slipped by.

At that moment the owl flew up and crashed through the cloth cover of the doorway, and the woman ran behind it, snatching her pullover and slippers as she moved.

Hamsa took a few steps outside the hut, half naked as he was, before stopping, clenching his fists, bitten with carnal pain.

The owl flew in a low circle around the corral and the shepherd's hut, before heading toward the cliffs. It flew against a strong wind, skirting the crags, toward the darkest part of the afternoon. It saw two falcons at the entrance of their nests in the crevice of the rock face. It stopped to rest on the roof of a small pink cottage that perched on a cliff over the sea. The wind was too strong to keep flying against it. There were people in the cottage. The owl launched itself into the emptiness and flew with the wind toward the light, dying now where the earth ended and there was only sea. It retraced its flight past the shepherd's hut, and, from on high, it could see the woman, who had put on her slippers and was walking hurriedly along the strip of grass bordering the asphalt road between the walls. The owl flew up as far as the summit and saw, in the distance, the glassy lights that lit up the hills, covered in a mantle of white houses fading into the folds of the parched and fissured countryside. It dipped down then, flying over the treetops toward a large abandoned house in the middle of a thick grove. It flew in through a window, greeted by the cries of the birds nesting there. It crossed through the house, flying from room to room through the hallways until it found an attic, with some roof tiles missing, the floorboards broken or completely rotten and a convenient cleft in the rough, dark wall.

NOTES

p. 5 Aid el Kebir—Muslim holy day, when sheep are slaughtered en masse, commemorating Abraham's willingness to sacrifice his son Isaac.

p. 5 Perdicaris—a rich Greek family, whose patriarch was kidnapped by Berbers in the early twentieth century.

p. 6 *Yalatif*—expression of despair, as in "God help us" or "My God!"

p. 7 gandura—hoodless, short-sleeved Moorish robe.

p. 8 Sidi Mesmudi—a religious sanctuary on Monte Viejo. (sidi: Sir, Lord.)

p. 10 *Hamdul-láh*—Praise be to Allah.

p. 10 *Shaitán*—Satan.

p. 16 *motui*—kif smoker's kit, containing the *sebsi* or kif pipe.

p. 23 *ouakha*—all right.

p. 27 Skulls—this is the literal meaning of *calaveras*, the Spanish word used here.

p. 43 "nobody in his right mind . . ."—common Moroccan belief.

p. 43 "Become who you are"—André Gide, *Les nouvelle nourritures*.

p. 43 *Báraca l-láh u fik*—God give you blessings.

p. 45 Djebel Musa—of the two pillars of Hercules, the one on the African shore; the other is Djebel Tarik (Arabic for Gibraltar).

p. 52 Polisario—the army in the old Spanish Sahara.

p. 60 *attup*—bear (Moroccan Arabic).

p. 61 B'slama—Goodbye (Moroccan Arabic).

p. 80 men were dogs—in the original Spanish, the word loosely translated here as "dogs" is *calaveras*, which literally means skulls but in Argentine slang refers to men devoted to pleasures of the flesh: playboys.

p. 81 *nabula*—kif container made of a sheep's bladder.

p. 86 Maghrebi—Moroccan Arabic. (The Arab name for Morocco was El-Maghrib or Moghreb el aksa: the farthest west.)

p. 89 *khay*—brother (Moroccan Arabic).

p. 90   *Intina yehudi!*—You are a Jew (a curse, Moroccan Arabic).

p. 96   *maquila*—practice of producing goods in a zone outside of the goods' trademark origin. (Cf. *maquiladora*, Mexican factories producing U.S. goods).

p. 127   *casheb*—a boy's long shirt.

p. 129   *Báraca*—a blessing.

AFTERWORD

Rodrigo Rey Rosa and Tangier

BY JEFFREY GRAY

Most of Rodrigo Rey Rosa's fifteen books of fiction are set in Guatemala; the exceptions are *Ningún lugar sagrado* (1998), a collection of nine short stories set in New York City; *The Good Cripple* (1996, translated into English in 2004), set in Guatemala and Morocco; *Que me maten si . . .* (1996), set in Guatemala, London, and Paris; and this book, *The African Shore* (La orilla africana, 1999), Rey Rosa's only novel set in Tangier.

To utter the word "Tangier" in a literary context is to invoke the American writer Paul Bowles, who lived in that city from the 1950s until his death in 1999, and who was Rey Rosa's mentor and friend, his first translator into English, and of whose literary estate Rey Rosa is heir. Many writers visited or frequented Tangier—Truman Capote, Tennessee Williams, Djuna Barnes, Alan Sillitoe, Allen Ginsberg, William Burroughs, among them—but only Bowles settled there for a lifetime. (He had first visited Tangier, with Aaron Copland, in the 1930s on the suggestion of Gertrude Stein.) In the context of *The African Shore*, it is worth reminding ourselves of the Bowles–Rey Rosa relationship and its importance for both writers.

In "Bowles y yo" (a title that alludes to Bowles's own "Bowles and It" as well as to Borges's prose poem "Borges y yo"), Rey Rosa tells how, at twenty-one, he saw a poster in the hallway of the School of Visual Arts in New York City advertising a "workshop" in Tangier; he signed up, and with fifty other Americans, most of them New Yorkers and most of them two or three times his age, flew to Tangier to study with Bowles.

Bowles himself recalled that experience:

> In the summer of 1980 I was conducting a workshop for "creative writing" at the American School of Tangier. The language used was English, since the students were Americans—with one exception. The youngest of the class was a Guatemalan, who wrote in Spanish. He had a fertile imagination, and used it to invent situations which were generally sinister. His texts were very short, often mere scenes or prose-poems of atmosphere, rather than tales, but all of them showed a power of invention capable of creating truly original situations.

During one of their earliest sessions, Bowles asked the class to name their favorite writers. When Rey Rosa mentioned Jorge Luis Borges, Bowles was pleased; he too had a predilection for Borges and had been the first to translate "The Circular Ruins" into English. After the session, Bowles told him he had traveled in Guatemala and knew Spanish, and advised Rey Rosa to write in Spanish thereafter. He also encouraged him to travel around Morocco; it wouldn't hurt to miss a few workshops, he said, especially since the discussions with the other students, writing in English, probably wouldn't be very helpful to his own work. Bowles lent him maps of northern Morocco to take with him, and Rey Rosa set off for the interior.

When Rey Rosa was about to return to New York, Bowles asked him if he would allow him to translate the stories (or prose poems) that the younger writer had handed in as coursework. A New York publisher (Red Ozier Press), specializing in "extravaganzas," had asked Bowles for a book for its catalogue, but he didn't have anything to send at the time. Could he translate Rey Rosa's stories and submit them? Thus began their long collaboration—asymmetrical, Rey Rosa notes, "since the student's translation of the master can't be on the same level as the master's translation of the student." (Bowles translated Rey Rosa's first three books, *Dust on Her Tongue*, *The Beggar's Knife*, and *The Pelcari Project*; Rey Rosa translated into Spanish Bowles's *Too Far from Home*, *Points in Time*, and *Selected Stories*, among others.)

■

The African Shore tells two stories, separate and yet so closely intertwined that one would be unintelligible without the other. (Indeed one was written in order to complement and complete the other.) The first is that of an adolescent Moroccan shepherd, Hamsa, who, having come down with a bad cold, is nursed back to health by his grandparents, who work at the villa of a wealthy Frenchwoman. The other concerns a young Colombian tourist who, having lost his passport during a night of drinking, uses this accident as an excuse not to return to his life in Colombia. While waiting for a new passport, buying kif, and courting a French archaeology student named Julie, he writes to and receives letters from his girlfriend in Cali, and we see him, day by day, letting that other life at "home" slip away.

The title *La orilla africana* could as easily be translated "the African bank," or "the African side," as opposed to the European side of the strait—that is, Gibraltar and Spain—or simply the European side of history. The title is not merely geographical. While a critique of empire is not foregrounded in *The African Shore*, the novel nonetheless touches on postcolonial themes: border crossing, transculturation, local corruption, illegal activity (smuggling), and the yawning chasm between the colonizer (whether tourist or French archaeologist) and the colonized. We know the time frame because "the fate of Pinochet" is a topic at the dinner table *chez* Mme. Choiseul, and Augusto Pinochet was detained in London between 1998 and 2000. The two "sides" are represented chiefly, as noted, by two characters: the tribal Hamsa, living in an animistic world he never questions, and the cosmopolitan Colombian tourist, unnamed until almost the novel's end, ready to sever all ties with his former life. The two worlds are not opposed but separate, their points of contact fleeting and incomplete.

Significantly, the moment that we finally learn the name of the Colombian protagonist is the very moment that he breaks out of the passivity that has enveloped him up to this point, eludes mortal danger, and starts, we imagine, a new life, one we will never know, though we sense that he stands on the first step of a long journey. The story of Hamsa is equally incomplete, though we suspect that the exotic possibilities placed in his mind by his uncle Jalid will remain there, not to be realized materially. Only the story of the owl—through whose eyes and ears we sometimes see and hear the world, *both* sides of it— offers a kind of closure. Only the owl, coveted by both sides— Christian and Muslim—achieves escape velocity.

From the beginning of his career, Rey Rosa diverged from the realist path taken by his fellow Guatemalan writers. His first books (especially the three that Paul Bowles translated) were written under the sign of Borges—cryptic, perhaps mystical ("Like many young men I was or thought I was a mystic," he remarks in an interview), economical, if not ascetic, and diaphanous. Of the stories in *Dust on Her Tongue*, Bowles said, "[They] are as compact and severe as theorems, eschewing symbol and metaphor, making their point in terse, undecorated statements which may bewilder the reader unaccustomed to such bareness of presentation." When asked how he shifted from this asceticism to the style and concept of his later fictions, Rey Rosa says that "it was a simple matter of writing longer works that made me try a different style. . . . The very brief stories tend toward prose poems, and in many cases benefited from a certain obscurity or hermeticism. On the other hand, in longer works obscurity becomes a defect. The urge toward clarity becomes an obligation." By the late 1990s he was moving toward realism, especially the subgenres of noir.

The African Shore seems to lie somewhere between these poles—telegraphic but grounded in material place and time, indeed based on concrete experience, hardly obscure but nevertheless ambiguous. (In common with the stories of Roberto Bolaño, the action in Rey Rosa's novel seems often to portend something that in fact may not occur.) Rey Rosa has said on this topic that one works to get precision and clarity, whereas complexity and ambiguity are matters more of the personality of the narrator, of the subjectivity. They are spontaneous or inevitable.

■

During the months prior to Bowles's death, Rey Rosa stayed in the Hotel Atlas. It was "an art deco building," he says, "and that's where I started to write the only one of my novels that takes place in Tangier, *La orilla africana.* It was winter and the heating in the Atlas never worked properly, so that when I was invited to spend the rest of my stay in a big 19th-century European house with large gardens in Monte Viejo, and with views of the cliffs that span both pillars of Hercules and the city of Tarifa set into the Spanish coast, I counted myself the luckiest Guatemalan in all Africa." Setting this account beside the novel, one sees immediately how much the latter owes to such lived details, which frame the situation of the Colombian protagonist: the big European house and its garden, Monte Viejo, the Marshan, the European residences on the outskirts, Sidi Mesmudi, even the eucalyptus in the fireplace. *La orilla africana* is saturated in the atmosphere of Tangier and its environs—not in the layered way of a Graham Greene novel or a Bruce Chatwin travel book, but in Rey Rosa's signature blend of rigor, ellipsis, and specificity.

Rey Rosa spent his last long residence in Tangier in 1998. "Hassan II had just died," he writes, "and his son was going to bring many changes, most of them purely cosmetic. But changes in the outside world had also affected Tangier—one saw women police in the streets, shanty towns of Moroccans from the interior had sprung up, along with ghettos of immigrants from other parts of Africa, who made Tangier their last stop before launching their assault on the fortress of Europe. The city had changed so much compared to the Tangier of the 1980s that one might repeat what Bowles wrote comparing the city he'd known in the '30s with that which came to be in the '50s: 'the only thing that remains is the wind.'"

Rey Rosa ends his memoir of Bowles as he began it, with a dream: it is after the American writer's death, and his books are being burned. Rey Rosa thinks it's a cremation, but then he and Abdelouahaid, Bowles's long-time assistant, hear a scream, coming from a metal bust of Bowles. They run into the fire and push some buttons on the neck and back of the bust, which opens up to reveal the old and frail Bowles himself. They carry him through the flames, out through the lobby, "where one can see the Tangerine night full of stars and the ghostly roman cypresses beyond the big gate of the Monte Viejo mansion with its Moorish arch standing wide open."

In its cadence and mystery, as well as in its final image (with that mixture of "clarity and enigma" that the Catalán writer Pere Gimferrer has noted in *La orilla africana*), this record of the end of a dream may remind one of the ending of the novel itself, set as it is on a fault line between cultures and continents: the owl flying through the now open door, seizing the long-awaited chance to circle beyond the African and European sides, and to find its perch in a distant and undetermined place.

RODRIGO REY ROSA is perhaps the most prominent writer on the Guatemalan literary scene. Along with the work of writers like Roberto Bolaño, Horacio Castellanos Moya, and Fernando Vallejo, Rey Rosa's fiction has been widely translated and internationally acclaimed. His books include *Dust on Her Tongue*, *The Beggar's Knife*, and *The Pelcari Project*, all of which were translated into English by the late Paul Bowles. In addition to his many novels and story collections, Rodrigo Rey Rosa has translated books by Bowles, Norman Lewis, François Augiéras, and Paul Léautaud.

JEFFREY GRAY is author of *Mastery's End: Travel and Postwar American Poetry* and editor of the *Greenwood Encyclopedia of American Poets and Poetry*. He is also co-editor (with Ann Keniston) of *The New American Poetry of Engagement: A Twenty-First Century Anthology*. He is a professor of English at Seton Hall University in New Jersey.